RETURN FROM THE HOLLOW EARTH

War of the Inner Worlds

Other Books by the Authors

Book One: *The Hollow Earth: Revisited*
by Danny L. Weiss (2013)   320 p.

Book Two: *A Curious Pebble: The Hollow Earth and Pursuit of the Holy Lance* by David DiPietro Weiss and Danny L. Weiss (2017) 244 p.

There's Only One of us Here! A Guide for Aspiring Lightworkers
by David DiPietro Weiss (2012)   127 p.

Impressions from Yonder Soul: Truth & Belief / Choice & Intuition
by David DiPietro Weiss (2015)   70 p.

The Musings of Consciousness: Collected Writings by David DiPietro
Weiss (2017)   182 p.

Voices From Within

David DiPietro Weiss SoulTalk series   36-44 p. $5.95

1 – *A Contract with your Soul / Rebirthing into Spirit* (2015)

2 – *The Dilemma of the Third Dimension / The Spiritual Laws of
Opportunity / Enlightenment* (2016)

3 – *Love, Actually / Possibility Consciousnesss / Astral-Energy Events /
The Spirit is Moved by Choice* (2016)

4 – *There is no God! / The Story of Haiku / Haiku poems* (2017)

5 – *Thoughts on Ethical Eating / The Foundation of Spiritual
Awakening* (2017)

6 – *Free Will: Truth or Wishful Thinking? / Why Do We Write? /
Poems from the Soul* (2017)

7 – *Illusion / Salt of the Earth: A Song for My Father* (2017)

RETURN FROM THE HOLLOW EARTH

War of the Inner Worlds

David DiPietro Weiss

with Danny L. Weiss

Cover Design by Melanie Gendron

Reptilian image by Melanie Gendron

Printed in the United States of America

ISBN 978-1-952194-02-3

To order additional copies please visit:

www.riversanctuarypublishing.com

RIVER SANCTUARY PUBLISHING
P.O Box 1561
Felton, CA 95018
www.riversanctuarypublishing.com
Dedicated to the awakening of the New Earth

Acknowledgments

No book is ever written without substantial contributions from others. This book is no exception.

I want to first recognize and thank Annie Elizabeth, my spouse and companion, for her edits, rewrites, and continual encouragement in finishing this treatise. I dedicate this book to her. As the CEO of our joint venture, River Sanctuary Publishing, she has been the rock and example of what it takes to complete such a project.

My co-conspirator and brother, Danny L. Weiss, was an integral part of the writing. His ability to create and push the dialogue was essential in our quest to write a sequel to *A Curious Pebble*.

I am also eternally grateful to Adra Ross, who has been my friend, proofreader, editor and critic for much of my writing. Her contributions gave continuity and purpose to each chapter while advising on structure and evntual content. Thank you, Adra!

Markos Moreno, my wife's youngest son, a talented artist and contributor, was my brainstorming partner who suggested several incidents compiled in the book. His ideas flowed freely into areas that many would not attempt to approach.

There is always someone who appears that continually heartens one to keep working and developing one's writing. Annelise Schinzinger, a published author in her own right, was always present at the right moments to prod me into completing the work. Her encouragement was essential to the psyche of this author.

Finally, one cannot exaggerate the contribution of our graphic artist, Melanie Gendron, an accomplished painter, illustrator, and designer. Her art is well known and she crossed into incredibly creative territory while designing the cover and developing the drawings of an alien humanoids for this book. She has developed artwork for each of my publications and an acknowledgement of her expertise is gratifying and humbling.

Contents

INTRODUCTION

*J*t was the Earth calendar year of 1987 when two significant events would occur on our beloved blue planet within the solar system we think of as our universe. Scientists, sages, and spiritual teachers from all walks and schools of spirit greeted the perpendicular alignment of the nine planets within our system as a significant milestone in the evolution of our local cosmos. *The Harmonic Convergence*, as it was called, set into motion a worldwide flurry of scientific and spiritual exploration, birthing a shift in understanding and an inquiry into the human dimensions beyond the finite limits of our heretofore known reality.

The other incident, one not chronicled with any notable publicity, was the impending return to the surface world from the middle Earth of two young sojourners who had fled through the North polar opening to return the powerful *Holy Lance* to the *Arianni*, the inhabitants of the Hollow Earth.

The saga of the Holy Lance, known historically as the *Spear of Longinus*, became the crux and focal point of subsequent history. The Spear that Longinus employed as a Roman Centurian was honed to perfection as a treasured heirloom handed down from generation to generation in his family. In accordance with the practice of the time, Longinus pierced the side of Jesus while on the cross to determine whether he still was alive. The emergence of fluid from the ribcage of Jesus indicated that he was not yet dead. In an act of mercy, Longinus spared Jesus the Roman ritual of breaking the legs of the still-living accused, cutting them down and clubbing them. Granting this reprieve was the sole decision of Longinus. He was revered as a great hero, and later was called a saint by a community of the first Christians in Jerusalem. Longinus was the prime witness to the shedding of the blood and the making of a new covenant for which the Spear of Destiny became the symbol.

Longinus, also known as Gaius Cassius and as an elder Roman Centurion, had been directed by Pontius Pilate in the months preceding the crucifixion to follow and observe the activities of Jesus, suspected to be a threat to the sanctity of the Roman Empire. Pilate determined that Jesus was, indeed, a threat after hearing the reports of the mass healings drawing crowds numbering in the thousands. Pontius Pilate condemned Jesus to die on the cross. However, in the course of his surveillance duty, Longinus became convinced that Jesus was a healer and an emissary of Divine love. As a loyal Centurian, however, Longinus followed orders and carried out the death sentence.

After the death of Longinus, the Spear became a holy relic, sought after and possessed by a remarkable series of monarchs and oligarchs through the ensuing centuries.[1] The Holy Lance was believed to hold mystical power, carrying with it the ominous mantra:

> *Whosoever possesses this Holy Lance*
> *and understands the power it serves,*
> *holds the destiny of the world for good or evil.*

Consequently, the Lance was passed down through many historical leaders, each seeking to harness the power of the Lance, each not fully understanding or succeeding in utilizing the inherent power of the Spear of Destiny. The legend continued unabated until the Lance was seized by Adolf Hitler, who, as a young man, became enamored with the Spear and its mystical legend when it was displayed in Vienna, Austria. After Hitler's ascension to the Chancellorship of Germany in 1933, he confiscated the mystical spear from a Vienna museum. Hitler sought to employ the power embedded within the rich legend of the Lance to accomplish his dream of the Nazi Third Reich.[2]

These significant celestial and human events, however, many years after the possession of the Lance by Hitler, concurrently opened the gates of new exploration and realization of the perils and promises of the new millennium, both on Earth and within the solar system.

Return From The Hollow Earth: War Between the Inner Worlds is the sequel to *A Curious Pebble: The Hollow Earth and Pursuit of the Holy Lance*, published in 2017. The screenplay of *A Curious Pebble* was renamed *Escape to the Hollow Earth* and has won numerous worldwide awards for best new Science Fiction screenplay. (See www.EscapeToHollowEarth.com)

As we left our young champions, they had just escaped from Spitzbergen, Norway, to the center of the Earth, eluding the clutches of the pursuing Ritters of the Ancient Order of Teutonic Knights,[3] with the liberated Holy Lance in their possession. Their mission was to return the Holy Lance to its spiritual home – that is, to the Arianni population of the Hollow Earth.

Over a decade has passed since our heroes, Gugga and Garrett, escaped from the Teutonic Knights and their malevolent attempt at establishing a Fourth German Reich with Garrett as their supposed faux titular leader. They entered the subterranean city of Agartha after escaping to the Hollow Earth on Admiral Richard E. Byrd's ancient Fokker tri-motor aircraft, cared for over thirty years by Sven Olaffson, an emissary of the Arianni inner Earth dwellers.

It was Loki, Sven's pet polar bear, who diverted the attention of the pursuing Teutonic Knights after they held Garrett and Gugga captive. The huge animal burst into Sven's antiquated Spitzbergen hangar, snatching the Holy Lance and holding it tightly clenched in his powerful jaws as he ran away from the group and disappeared into the adjacent Nordic ice floes. The unexpected encounter with Loki panicked the startled Teutonic troupe and provoked them into chasing after the bear to retrieve the Holy Lance.

During the commotion that ensued, Sven assisted Garrett and Gugga by providing their means to escape during the confusion, firing up the ancient Fokker aircraft and preparing it for takeoff. Sven had fashioned a substitute Holy Lance that Loki had snatched, while the authentic Lance remained in his possession.

Garrett and Gugga thus escaped the malicious plans of the Knights who were determined to co-opt Garrett, who saw through the Teutonic plot, as the Arianni's chosen successor of the Spear of Longinus, to implement their assumed assured destiny of an intended Fourth Reich.[4]

Leaving behind the Ritters marooned on breaking ice floes as they pursued Sven's runaway polar bear with the Holy Lance firmly in its teeth, Gugga and Garrett took advantage of the confusion and flew triumphantly off in Admiral Byrd's vintage Fokker Tri-motor, in possession of the genuine Holy Lance.

As they flew unknowingly through an Arctic U.S No-fly zone, Garrett and Gugga were confronted by U.S. Air Force jets who had been commanded to shoot down any violators of the restricted air space. At the same moment that they were supposedly blasted out of the sky by the interceptors, a flugelrad (flying saucer) appeared, surprisingly piloted by Garrett's missing Viet-Nam era brother, Jared. Jared attached a curious tractor-beam that guided the plane through the polar opening to the subterranean land of the Arianni. Our sojourners were lowered through the polar opening to Agartha, the inner Earth capital city. Here they were met by Thal, the leader of the Arianni, a seemingly ethereal and somewhat mysterious acquaintance who had previously appeared to both Garrett and his father Ollie in impressive fashion. Thal welcomed them warmly and invited them to stay for a period of time until they were trained in the ways of the Arianni and the means of utilizing the power of the Holy Lance. They would then be educated and trained to contribute to the critical peace process on the surface world.

Agartha is a vast underground world terminal city with many branches of subterranean and sub-oceanic networks of tunnels and vacuum-assisted magnetic transportation tubes leading to several destinations within the inner civilization.

The highly emotional regret of Garrett and Gugga was the necessity of leaving behind Thora, their pre-teen daughter, in the care of her grandparents. Thora was to wait for her parents to return, having no idea how long the wait would be. Eventually, a MIB[5] emissary from the Arianni Hollow Earth dwellers delivered the actual Holy Lance to her, indicating that her parents were safe and portending a future role and mission for Thora.

While in Agartha, also known as Asgarth, Garrett and Gugga are informed of an immediate threat to peace within the Galaxy through information garnered from the knowledge and wisdom of the Arianni. Their potential mission back to the surface world takes on a wider meaning as they discover a greater immediate crisis threatening both the inner and surface Earth from the humanoid reptilian Inner planet dwellers of Venus, an alien race known as the Annunaki.

It is here that our story continues.

---

[1]   After the siege and capture of the city of Acre in 1191, **Duke Leopold of Austria** quarreled with the *powerful King Richard of England* and decided that the lance should be hidden in some secret place. *In that year, a secret organization of crusaders formed the Teutonic Knights, or Knights of the Teutonic Order.* Leopold placed the Lance in their custody. Richard of England forced Leopold to quit the Crusade and come home. (See Appendix I).

[2]   After the fall of the 3rd Reich, the Lance, along with Hitler's ashes and other Nazi artifacts were transported by the submarine U-530 to a cave embedded within the Mülig-Hofmann Mountains in Antarctica. They were returned to Germany in 1978 to be sequestered securely at Wewelsburg Castle near Westphalia, West Germany. The castle was also the home of the Nazi 4th and 5th dimension occult sojourns led by Heinrich Himmler. (The First Reich [empire] was considered the Holy Roman Empire 962 – 1806; The Second Reich was the German Empire 1871 – 1918; The 3rd Reich was the Nazi domination from 1933 -1945.)

[3]   Ritter: Germanic term for Knight.

[4]   Rightful successor is Garrett as determined by the Arianni through the work of the Teutonic Knights.

[5]   MIBs, or Men in Black, are biologically engineered robots who are characteristically dressed in 1950's era black suits, always wearing dark sunglasses to hide their blue eyes with striking vertical pupils. They are emissaries of the Hollow Earth sent on various missions on the surface to gather information or deliver messages to the Earth dwellers.

PRELUDE

*T*he tightening pressure of the alien's tentacles pressed against her neck had Thora panicking with the fear of losing consciousness and dying. She struggled to maintain her power, but felt her resistance waning as the creature intensified its grip. Her whole body went limp as her strength seemed to evaporate leaving little hope of survival.

As she began to plummet into darkness, she felt the effect of a sharp blow against the creature's neck that caused it to release her as she collapsed on the floor. In the corner of her eye appeared the image of her father, who somehow had appeared and dealt a striking blow with the Holy Lance to the alien reptilian creature's head, causing it to free her from certain death. She collected what strength she had and embraced her father as he held her and caressed her within his protective arms.

"I've got you, dear daughter, you're safe now."

"Daddy, Daddy! You've come at last. I've missed you so," she sobbed with a mixture of relief, surprise, and delight.

****

Thora bolted upright in her bed. She rubbed her eyes, cloudy from the abrupt awakening, and stared at the Lance hanging on her bedroom wall. It was, again, the dream – a dream that had occurred many times since parting from her parents some years ago as they entered the middle Earth. Her angst had haunted her every day since their departure.

She had, on occasion, shared her frightening rescue dream with Ollie and Jackie, her grandparents, who had kindly taken her in to live with them after the heart-wrenching separation. Both continued to offer understanding, emotional support, and love to their grand-daughter, aware of the anxiety she held deep within. Yet Thora knew that only the return of her parents could dissipate the specter of this recurring event.

Chapter 1

FROM RAGGS TO UC

*T*he University of California at Berkeley had always loomed as Thora's first choice to attend due to the high academic standards and reputation of the institution. Of course, growing up in the proximity of the campus gave the young woman access to many educational, artistic, and cultural opportunities that existed in this iconic northeastern San Francisco Bay City, enticing her with the promise of fulfilling her academic dreams.

Thora planned to enter as a freshman in this prestigious school and further pursue her childhood interest in geology. Already a substantial self-taught academic in the field, her time in California forged an unbreakable yearning to deepen her expertise as she read volumes of books and articles containing theories and information on her favorite subject. She was excited to begin student life with professionals in the field as she envisioned expanding her already ample geological knowledge.

Her first day of class in geology, however, proved to be a disappointment. As the professor introduced the syllabus for the class, it became apparent that Thora was much more advanced in the study than virtually all of her fellow students. The instructor seemed to cater to the lowest common knowledge base and proposed to teach the course with facts and theories that Thora had long ago mastered and moved beyond. Not once did she hear anyone mention or suggest that the stones they studied had ethereal qualities.

"Perhaps," she thought to herself, "I chose the wrong academic pursuit to continue my education."

After giving the course a chance to expand its challenge for a month while personally experiencing a dramatic increase in boredom, Thora decided that she would need to augment her next semester's classes by exploring an entirely different field of study. Her self-learned knowledge in the field of geology was more expansive than she had realized. Her inquisitive mind hungered for new inspiration.

Thora spent a great deal of time at the extraordinary University library, which seem to have everything a student would ask for in pursuing virtually any academic subject. As she browsed through the stacks, she would occasionally pull a book on an unfamiliar topic and scan it for a possible spark of new interest.

It was in the bookstacks on the fourth floor that she first noticed a tall, young Nordic man browsing much like she was, but in a particular section catering to a subject she had not heard of before. She watched him discreetly as he gathered several books on Artificial Intelligence[1] and carried them off to a secluded table near the library window. This same occurrence took place over the next several days where both of them converged in the library, the young man repeating his habits, focused on his study.

Thora noticed a few books that he had put back on the shelves after pouring over them at his usual station by the window. She quietly and discreetly approached the shelf and took down one of the books entitled, *Essentials of Artificial Intelligence*, and brought it back to her study table. With her interest and courses in computer technology, Thora quickly became fascinated with the premises of the field and, over the next week, perused a few more books on the subject. As Thora became more and more intrigued by A.I, as it was called, she sought to gather the courage to ask the young man more about what he gleaned from his readings. Alas, however, by the time she decided to approach him, he apparently had completed his research at the library and, much to her chagrin, she didn't see him again.

What Thora didn't know, however, was that the young man had noticed her as well. At first he was drawn by her blonde hair cascading down over her shoulders, but on successive days he became captivated by the aura of deep focus and strength that surrounded her. He considered approaching her, but she appeared to be too involved in her research to be disturbed. And similarly, Raggnar Raggnesson found himself too deeply involved with his own studies to initiate a conversation. Admittedly, he felt some regret that he had not seized the opportunity to speak to this intriguing young lady.

As the weeks passed and the initial semester came to an end, Thora had decided to explore the subject of artificial intelligence and signed up for two classes in the field. The direction of this entirely new field of study awakened her imagination and would require her to enhance her growing computer skills. Computers were just beginning to assert their prominence at academic institutions and inasmuch as they presented another challenge to Thora, she enthusiastically plunged into the study with the gusto she exhibited in her past studies of geology. She spent many an hour after her computer classes exploring the world of computers and artificial intelligence. She had found a new passion.

As fate would dictate, on the first day of a class in AI she had registered for, she entered the lecture hall and was astonished to find the young man she remembered from the library standing in front of the class at the podium. She smiled to herself, feeling delighted to see him again and at the same time appreciating his role as teacher for the class. As he glanced around the lecture hall to catch the faces of his students, Ragnaar Raggnesson noticed the lovely Thora sitting a few rows from the front. His eyes fixed on her for a moment before he introduced himself to the class and launched into his subject for the day.

A week later, Thora was working on a computer in the lab when Raggnar came over to greet her.

"I remember you from the library," he said rather crisply, attempting to respect his relationship with a student in his class. "Most folks call me Raggs, not Professor Raggnesson. I'm not really a professor," he said sheepishly, "but was hired as a part-time teaching assistant. I'm actually a third year grad student trying to hone my skills in artificial intelligence. I don't want to represent myself as more than that. I know your name is Thora, from my roll sheet. That's an unusual name in this country."

"Hello," Thora responded with a wide smile, "I'm pleased to see you here. In fact it was you who kindled my interest in this class. I watched you gathering AI books in the library and, I have to admit, I was curious and perused some of the books you had been working with. I became interested in the subject, and here I am."

"Wow, that's quite a complement. It's flattering to know I may have inspired you in some way."

"Well, I'm enjoying the class and I am delighted to meet you informally," she retorted, continuing her inviting smile.

"And yes, it is an unusual name in America. I am originally from Iceland and have been here for just a few years."

"Iceland! I too am from Iceland!" Raggs replied excitedly. "I left some years ago with the intent of coming here to go to school. I graduated two years ago and am staying on to complete my master's degree and doctorate in artificial intelligence. What a happy coincidence!"

Thora was taken by this young man's warmth and enthusiasm. He was a tall, good-looking, sandy-haired blonde with prominent Nordic features that she recognized as probably a native of the Scandinavian region, but was surprised and delighted to learn that he was a kindred soul from Iceland. She thought to herself that they might have much in common and looked forward to possibly developing a rapport on a more casual level. After all, he was only a few years older than she – but she was aware that having a personal connection with one of her teachers could put both of them at risk in a relationship. She quickly dismissed the thought as Raggs accepted her invitation to sit down and join her.

Thora and Ragnaar enthusiastically exchanged remembrances and experiences of their respective lives in Iceland. Both were born near Reykjavik, but did not recognize any connections between their respective families. They simply seemed to enjoy one another as the conversation morphed into school thoughts and light personal exchanges.

It was getting late into the afternoon when Thora noticed the time had passed more quickly than she has anticipated. She gracefully ended the conversation, letting Raggs know that her grandparents were expecting her home.

Ragnaar rose as Thora stood up and extended his hand to her to bid goodbye. He said he hoped they could meet again more informally after the semester ended. She pondered the impact of his words and simply uttered, "I'd like that," accepting his gesture by placing her hand in his while rising from the table. She turned and, with some reluctance, left the library.

****

Thora arrived back at her grandparents home just in time to sit down to a dinner that Jackie had prepared to commemorate Thora's first full day of semester classes at the university. Jackie had spent the afternoon baking a sumptuous rum cake, a family favorite, as well as a three course feast. Ollie and Jackie Hill, Thora's grandparents, represented home to her, as she had taken residence with them immediately after her parents embarked on their sojourn into the center of the Earth. Thora settled into the warmth of the room, feeling grateful that her grandparents allowed her the flexibility and encouragement to follow her dreams. The crux of her dreams, of course, centered on the return of her parents, but also included the prospect of learning all she could while attending the university.

"How was your day today, my dear," queried Jackie as she meticulously spooned her special mixture of vegetables and broth of a deliciously pungent mushroom based soup.

"I had a marvelous day," Thora enthusiastically responded. "I have great classes, and today I met with one of my teachers while in the library. He was very nice and comes from Iceland," she cooed. "We spent well over an hour sharing thoughts about Iceland. It was very exciting. He was extremely handsome, very intelligent, and probably only four or five years older than me."

"Hmmm," Jackie responded, "He sounds interesting," shifting her eyes towards her husband, Ollie, to see if he picked up the excitement in her tone.

Ollie wasn't paying rapt attention, as he was settling down in his chair glancing at his plate, appreciating the first course of the lavish meal his wife was serving.

"Did anyone hear the news today?" he queried. "It seems that the President is arranging a potential disarmament conference with the Russians. It seems as if Mikhail Gorbachev, the Soviet leader, is creating some negotiation room with what is anticipated to be a welcome proposal."

Neither Thora nor Jackie responded, as each was fabricating their own vision of the chance meeting with a handsome young man that had taken place today. Ollie seemed oblivious to the happening. Jackie recognized the first signs of attraction for Thora who, up to now, had not seemed very interested in boys, even as they hovered around her throughout high school drawn by her beauty, but intimidated by her intelligence.

Thora's choice of a new major, artificial intelligence, commonly referred to as AI, opened wide, new vistas of opportunity, research and practice that tweaked the curiosity of this gifted young woman. The potential of an emerging relationship with Raggnar obviously contributed to her enthusiasm, especially coupled with a new-found interest in computers and their academic relationship with AI, chemistry, and biology.

As a dedicated student, Thora became immersed in the study of artificial intelligence. She marveled at the potential that the field offered. Her blossoming association with Raggs, no doubt, contributed to her profound interest. Even as AI was still in the early stage of development, Thora sought to expand the inquiry related to the field to include a biological component. Up to this point, in the new age of computers, AI was limited to smart engineering and making intelligent machines, especially intelligent computer programs. She felt, however, that AI should not have to confine itself to that which was scientifically observable.

Thora's interest in a biological component to artificial intelligence was keyed by her knowledge of the biologically engineered robots that her father and she had encountered, often known as Men in Black (MIBs). She had had a direct encounter with such an entity a year or so ago when one of them came to her door posing as a postal employee to deliver the Holy Lance into her hands. Thora knew the MIBs came from the inner Earth, as Ollie had discussed his encounters with her and Jackie on many occasions, and was captivated by the prospect of knowing how they were created.

She shared her experiences with Raggs as he became energized about the potential biological breakthrough in AI that the MIBs might represent. He had no problem believing that they existed, as their authenticity was a closely guarded secret in his home country of Iceland. Together they immersed themselves into the study, forming an intriguing and blossoming, personal bond emanating from their joint interest.

---

[1] Artificial intelligence (AI) as it is known, was founded as an academic discipline in 1956. In the subsequent years AI has experienced several waves of optimism and disappointment. Intelligence by machines, rather than humans or animals, became the goals of computer programmers in AI since that time. English mathematician Alan Turing, one of the original founders of the study (he cracked the German enigma code during WWII) started to work on intelligent machines and may have been the first to decide that AI was best researched by programming computers rather than by building machines. By the late 1950s, there were many researchers on AI and most of them were focusing their work on programming computers.

Chapter 2

THE WAIT IS OVER!

*T*hora was now twenty-four years old, an honor graduate from the University of California, Berkeley, with specialties in Artificial Intelligence, Computer Science, Geology, and Biology. She had not seen her parents for over a dozen years and, even though she intuitively and telepathically knew that they were safe, she puzzled as to why they had not as yet returned. Thora resolved that she would be patient and have faith that all was well. Her life would go on.

****

The amusement park atmosphere was accentuated by the circus-sounding calliope permeating the grounds of the Alameda County Fair near the San Francisco Bay town of Pleasanton, California. Carnival rides and game booths were scattered amongst the specialty acts and events that the day featured. Adjacent to the midway attractions were acres of buildings and displays of various types of fruits, vegetables, flowers, and homemade specialties that created a healthy array of farmer's wares and exhibits. People of all ages, sizes, and shapes dotted the landscape, each displaying their own unique attire celebrating the annual event.

The fair had become an annual grandmother/granddaughter event for Thora and Jackie, and they looked forward to the frivolity and spectacle of the attendees and displays. It was always a special time for each of them as both found interest and fascination with the diversity of the exhibitions. Jackie was drawn to the unique tapestry of quilts, sewing innovations, as well as homey displays of pies, jams, and culinary delights . Thora, on the other hand, gravitated towards the gem and rock displays as well as any geological model displays of mountains, lakes, landscapes, and valleys. Each would accompany the other, often strolling hand in hand, their hearts warmed by the sharing of one another's knowledge and interests.

After satisfying themselves with the ample food offerings available throughout the fair, soaring in the heart-stopping heights of the Ferris wheel and participating in other booth activities, they eventually settled down at an available outside picnic table where they joyfully observed and commented on the myriad of characters in attendance at the fair.

Thora, raised in Iceland, had completely integrated her life with that of her American grandparents since the time over a decade ago when her parents, Garrett and Gugga, had entered the Hollow Earth to return the Holy Lance to the Arianni. She had adjusted well and embraced the active American lifestyle. Now in her early 20s, she felt completely at home with the love and support of her attentive grandparents. While enjoying her life, she held in her heart a recurring vision that one day soon she would welcome her parents back from their adventure within the Earth.

Thora had carried this secret with her without hinting to anyone the plight of her parents. Because of this she found it difficult to have close friends. After all, what would they think about such a fantastical story? Thora would often meditate in the sanctuary of her room, gazing at the prized Holy Lance still in her possession. On these occasions she would tune in and often receive vague telepathic communications from her mother which reinforced her intuitive knowing that her parents were safe and would return when the time was right. In the meantime, Thora immersed herself in her education and ranked high in her academic pursuits. She was no longer a little girl, no longer a naïve teenager, but had grown to be a beautiful, intelligent, and athletic young woman – much in the image of her mother. She was smart, aware, observant, and seemed different, somewhat more mature, than other young women her age. Earlier that summer she had received her MS, (Master of Science) degree at the University of California, Berkeley, the highly prestigious West Coast academic institution. Her specialty majors were in artificial intelligence and computer applications. Her accumulated knowledge and experience in geology helped round out her academic pursuits. She was aware of and demonstrated unusual powers of intuitive clairvoyance that had enhanced her spiritual thinking and knowledge far beyond that of her peers.

Today, however, promised to be a landmark day for Thora. As was her passion when she attended outside events, she would generally gravitate towards the displays of gems and stones, drawn by both an academic and personal intuitive spiritual interest. Her interest had become an obsession over the years and her personal excitement when handling the gems and stones was palpable. Touching and handling each stone produced within her a healing and spiritual vibration that had given her unique insights, powers, and second-sighted visions of events that defied logic and practice. Part of her ability of clairvoyance was activated within her by the different vibrations of each stone. She had been very careful not to reveal these inner powers to anyone, not even her grandparents or parents, although all seemed to be acutely aware of her special abilities – yet choosing not to reveal their observations out of respect for Thora.

They patiently awaited the time they knew would come when Thora would be ready to share her secrets with them.

As she opened her eyes to a new day, Thora recalled the peculiar morning of her 18th birthday, nearly six years ago, waking from a recurring dream. Her gaze was fixed upon the wall-mounted Holy Lance that was delivered to her by the eerie MIB on that eventful morning sometime after her parents, Garrett and Gugga, had entered the middle Earth. She had immediately placed it over her vanity and mounted it securely with wood screws. As a reminder of the significance of the artifact, she added the historical statement that she had stylishly mounted on a California Redwood plaque, remembering the proclamation associated with the Lance. It read,

Whosoever possesses this Holy Lance
and understands the power it serves,
holds the destiny of the world for good or evil.

She recollected her bizarre behavior that early birthday morning with a quizzical smile knowing that her performance was entirely off the wall. She was relieved that Grandpa Ollie and Grandma Jackie had no knowledge of it.

As she recalled, she awoke with excitement that birthday morning of August 19th 1987, exhibiting her typical sparkling, enthusiastic, demeanor. She bounced about in her high energy mood preparing for school. She remembered standing in front of the large full-length oval mirror in the corner of her bedroom sharply glancing back and forth at the ancient spear collecting dust on the wall of her bedroom. It had been there since the mysterious Man in Black presented it to her when she was much younger.

She recalled brushing her long blonde hair wildly with hasty and abrupt motions. Unsatisfied with her appearance, she tossed the brush in the vanity drawer and slammed it closed while pulling out another drawer searching for additional things for her hair. Immediately she changed her mind and tossed it all back into the drawer. She again slammed the drawer shut in frustration.

She turned, lividly glancing back at the Spear again and again before staring at it with deep intensity. While turning her attention to her image in the mirror, she placed her right hand against her right hip with her elbow pointing outwards.

Assuming a conqueror's posture, Thora spoke aloud and with conviction quoting words from Napoleon Bonaparte, speaking in French, as if she were a female warrior and tyrannical conqueror. "Death is nothing," she stated emphatically, "but to live defeated and ingloriously is to die daily." She sprang back towards the Lance and jerked it from its encasement.

Thora chuckled as she remembered the sequence of her actions that morning. She had imagined herself as the many conquerors that laid claim to the Lance and swore allegiance to its supreme power. She then shouted out, "It is she! Not he! It is SHE who holds this spear and understands its powers and serves the destiny of the world for good or evil!"

Swept away in her impassioned declarations, she continued to imagine herself as other historical conquerors and momentarily saw faded manifestations of them appear within her visage, seemingly trapped behind her own reflection in the mirror.

She paraded around her bedroom mimicking Julius Caesar and orating his words through an unconscious memory, exclaiming, "*Veni Vidi Vici*! I came, I saw, I conquered. It is better to create than to learn. Creating is the essence of life."

The impromptu drama seemed to unfold with an energy of its own as Thora again grabbed her hairbrush and positioned it above her upper lip, imagining it to be the moustache of Adolf Hitler as she shook the Lance up and down staring staunchly into the mirror proclaiming with a silly German accent, "Who says that I am not under special protection of God?"

Somewhat exhausted by her passionate and emotional display, Thora again raised the spear up and down above her head. In an unusually loud, cracking, and frustrated voice, she blurted out, "I've been staring at this thing for years. Why in God's name do I have this, and what am I supposed to do with it? Maybe it's just a broomstick with a sharp point! What magic power does it have?"

She relaxed, composed herself and mumbled, "What good can I possibly do for this Earth? I'm just a girl, a female, and no one ever listens to girls. Hmmm . . ." she paused thoughtfully and declared, "Maybe they'll listen now that I hold the Lance."

Back in present time, Thora momentarily glanced again at herself in the mirror, instantly dismissing the whole act and pondering with amusement her childish behavior of her 18th year.

****

Thora cleared her mind of her recurring morning dreams and dressed to meet the new day. She was excited to attend the yearly fair with her beloved grandmother, Jackie. Just on the outskirts of the midway was located a booth with an annual display of hundreds of beautiful gems, stones, crystals, and rocks. Some were small and polished, but many were larger and split open to reveal colorful crystals inside. Each of them, at least to Thora, had a story to tell and a power to share. She had been aware of the language of stones since she was a little girl – collecting samples along with her Icelandic friend, Meda.

As she matured, the messages seemed to become much clearer and Thora deepened her capacity to communicate with the energy in the stones. She and Meda enjoyed occasional communications with one another, mostly by letter, but increasingly by a new form of personal contact – email. Meda admired Thora's innate ability to read the sacred messages of the stones and was making some progress in her own attempts, spurred by Thora's remarkable insights.

Thora felt a surge of excitement as she approached the booth display. Sitting inside the booth, an intriguing woman was manipulating a large exposed amethyst with purple crystals jutting out from the center of the split stone, emitting a violet glow that reflected on the woman's face. Thora was impressed by the aura of serenity emanating from the woman and the peaceful loving smile that she displayed within her reflection. Thora stopped and stared at the scene, transfixed by the moment.

The woman opened her eyes slowly to find Thora looking intently and lovingly at her. She smiled at Thora and invited her to sit with her. Thora could not help but feel drawn to the woman's graceful face and peaceful demeanor. Her crystal blue eyes on her perfect and seamless facial countenance seemed other-worldly as she smiled, exposing her soft lips and strikingly perfect white teeth.

"My name is Solaris," she quietly said. "What is yours?"

Thora answered promptly and without hesitation as she felt an odd connection with this stranger, a stranger who displayed a comprehension of the vibrations of stones and seemed to communicate with them much like she did. Solaris was the first individual since Meda she had ever encountered who spoke and understood the language of the stones. There was something physically different about Solaris. At first, Thora could not pinpoint it, but soon realized the woman might not be from this planet. Her dolphin-like smile gave Thora an insight. Could she be an Arianni?

"And what does this beautiful Amethyst say to you, my dear?" Solaris quietly asked.

Thora paused for a moment and accepted the stone when Solaris handed it to her.

"It says I should be here at this moment, but I don't know why," Thora replied hesitantly.

Thora reverently placed the stone back into the outstretched hands of her new acquaintance. Solaris gazed deeply into the young woman's eyes, listening attentively.

"It is attempting to send me a message," Thora said, "and that the answer will be forthcoming."

Solaris smiled a knowing smile and softly caressed Thora's hands saying,

"Yes, there is a message for you."

As Thora pondered her reply, an unusually tall Nordic man from inside the booth appeared and acknowledged Thora.

"Hello Thora," the man said as he held out his hand in greeting. "I am Sven. I see you have already met Solaris."

"How do you know my name?" Thora replied.

"I've known you and who you are for many years," Sven responded.

Thora's heart took a leap. Yes, she knew him. No, she had never met him, but he was nonetheless a prominent figure in her life.

"You're Sven, aren't you? You're *that* Sven! You knew my parents. You know my grandfather! You helped my parents in their journey into the Earth! Didn't you?"

Sven smiled, nodding his head, revealing his prominent silver front tooth. He was the legendary figure that her grandfather, Ollie, often referred to when telling the story of Garrett's and Gugga's escape into the Hollow Earth.

"Ah yes, my dear Thora, Sven Olaffson. I have been waiting for you. We, together, have a mission to fulfill. It appears that now is the time for that undertaking. Are you ready to meet your parents again?"

Thora broke suddenly into tears. At last, the day she had been waiting for, the day that she had been promised so many years ago, was now at hand.

"Yes, yes," she sobbed. "I have been waiting for you. This is my destiny!"

Jackie, who had been at the adjoining booth admiring some paintings and drawings, was shocked to look over and see her granddaughter in tears.

She quickly rushed over and exclaimed, "My dear, what is the matter? Are you all right?" Jackie took Thora into her arms to comfort her as both Solaris and Sven stood by, both smiling.

"What's going on here?" Jackie asked quietly.

Sven extended his hand towards Jackie, displaying a big grin and introduced himself.

"Hello, Mrs. Hill. My name is Sven Olafsson. I'm an old friend of your husband . . . and your son and daughter-in-law. We shared a significant adventure together in Spitzbergen, Norway a few years back. And this is my companion, Solaris, an Arianni and resident of the inner Earth."

Jackie was dumbfounded. Her present had just been invaded by the past and she was speechless as her mind raced through the stories that her husband, Ollie, had related to her about Gugga and

Garrett's flight to the polar opening. She, Ollie, and Thora had been waiting patiently for a sign when their son would return from the inner Earth and even as she realized that this was actually happening, all she could do was stand there in shock and awe.

After a few awkward moments, Jackie finally grasped the situation; that the wait, the agony, the continuing angst, was over. Both she and Thora embraced one another in tears as they struggled to regain their composure.

Sven finally broke the emotional tension and said, "We knew that Thora would find us here when the moment presented itself. I'm sorry it could not have been sooner, but the Arianni have been training your family to return to the surface world. I will be your contact until we arrange a meeting and reunion."

Handing them an innocuous business card, Sven assured Thora and Jackie that he would be contacting them soon. He let them know how anxious he was to meet with Ollie again and to send him his best wishes knowing they would meet very soon.

"I will be taking you to a very special place where we can relax in comfort and privacy. You will be able to spend some time with Garrett, Gugga, and Jared, who have been together within the Earth for the last few years. They are very excited and anxious to see you again."

"Jared, my son, Jared?" Jackie exclaimed. "He is with Garrett and Gugga? I can't believe it! I can't believe it!"

Sven smiled warmly and bid them good day as he and Solaris dismantled and closed the gem booth. They had accomplished their mission to attract and connect with Thora.

****

The Mercedes-Benz Limousine pulled up in front of the modest Berkeley home of Oliver and Jackie Hill. Jackie and Thora only yesterday afternoon had met with Sven and Solaris. Their account of the day at the fair was breathtakingly related to Ollie when they returned home, much to the eager ears of the now retired commander. Yes, he knew that one day this news would be forthcoming, but hearing of its reality ignited his anticipation and released the repressed aura of waiting patiently which he had exhibited in keeping with his typically patented, controlled emotions. The excitement he felt inside made him feel overjoyed and somehow fulfilled knowing, finally, that he would be seeing his two sons and Gugga again.

Sven had volunteered to drive them all, including Solaris, from Berkeley to the tiny Northern California town of Mt. Shasta, about a four hour drive north. There they would gain entrance to the subterranean Arianni city of Telos, situated deep under the great semi-extinct volcano that dominated the visual landscape for miles around. A reunion of epic proportions for the Hills would take place somewhere within the mythical inner Earth. When they would make the return trip home never entered any of their minds amid the excitement of the moment. That was the furthest thing from their thoughts.

A quick glimpse at the driver of the limo caused Ollie to chuckle, as one of the MIBs was at the wheel. Ollie remembered so very well the first appearances of these biologically engineered robots and how strange it had been for him. Now, of course, after a few serendipitous meetings over the years, Ollie found the humor in both his previous fears and misunderstandings. He was comfortable with the knowledge that Sven had everything very much in hand.

Chapter 3

SUBTERRANEAN CITY OF TELOS, MOUNT SHASTA

*T*he limo was unusually large and comfortable with seating for the five of them with, of course, the almost mechanical MIB driver. It was equipped with snacks and beverages and offered outstanding views of the countryside as well as breathtaking vistas through the clear and sliding roof hatch. The seats were plush and each had an individual lumbar and foot adjustment enabling all to ride in personal comfort. Safely resting next to Thora, wrapped in the original velvet cloth, was the Holy Lance that she had taken off her bedroom wall with the notion that she should return it to the Arianni. She would do that upon arrival in Telos.

Conversation on the journey was friendly and enthusiastic. All wanted to hear, again, Ollie and Sven's story of the escape from the Ritters, and especially the antics of Loki, Sven's well trained and loyal polar bear. As the story was relayed again with great pleasure, more and more questions about the details of the confrontation and flight were asked and addressed. Sven proved to be an excellent story teller, his front silver tooth displayed prominently while keeping his companions in ecstasy with his unique accent and colorful descriptions of the event. He relayed detailed incidents regarding Loki and the close relationship with his animal friend with creative facial expressions and comedic humor. Loki was healthy and doing well. He stayed often without Sven near the hanger in Spitzbergen, yet hanging out in his natural habitat, the ice floes, when Sven left for longer periods of time on errands for the Arianni. Once he sensed Sven's returns to the hangar, Loki would quickly leave the comfort of his ice wilderness and traipse enthusiastically back to greet his human companion with standing hugs and affection. Jackie and Thora delighted in Sven's expressions as Thora squealed in glee that she couldn't wait to meet Loki herself.

The time passed quickly with lively conversation. The road was unusually straight and the specter of the snow-covered Mount Shasta peak was becoming more and more prominent as they got closer. They turned off the main highway, Federal Route 5, and pulled into the small town of Mt. Shasta. The surrounding area was naturally beautiful, a seemingly untouched expanse of trees, boulders, volcanic rock, and shrubs typical of the sparsely populated inland Northern California environs.

The driver turned off the highway onto a twisty easterly road that led directly to the base of the majestic mountain, stopping at an impressive overlook next to a sheer granite wall. Sven, seated near the front of the limo, looked back at his entourage and explained to them the procedures they would be following to enter the mountain. He cautioned them not to be alarmed by any strange sounds or sensations of levitation they might experience.

Turning towards his entourage, Sven said with a reassuring tone, "The entry will confound you somewhat at first, but the journey will be comfortable and completed in just a few minutes."

With that introduction, Sven produced a small runic triangle[1] from his tunic that appeared to be slightly different than the make-shift one used by Garrett and Gugga to enable their escape from the Castle and entry to the polar opening. He placed an unfamiliar blue/green energizer stone that he wore around his neck in the center of the triangle and waited.

The outside sunshine immediately began to disappear behind a cloud cover that defied the warming day. A soft rumbling could be heard as the mountain wall opened as if by magic to reveal a cave-like entrance as the limo was engulfed in a cloudy mist. The mist was accompanied by a beam of light from the opening which attached itself to the automobile as a tractor beam. It transported the group into the bowels of the mountain down a darkened shaft, leaving them suspended over a crystal laden, tiered city of extraordinary beauty. The light beam gently brought the limo to a stop on a crystallized granite platform as a tandem of Arianni greeters approached the limo. They assisted the passengers out while preparing the group to board a transportation vehicle that would travel through a magnetic vacuum-assisted transit.

Known as *the Tube,* it was an engineering marvel that the Arianni[2] had developed over the centuries, consisting of many tunnel outlets and lines in and out of Agartha connecting the metropolis to all the other great cities and settlements within the inner Earth. The power source for the Tube employed powerful magnets in association with a hollow tube that utilized a complete vacuum space to provide smooth, effortless travel for all. The Tube was used constantly to whisk the Hollow Earth citizens to and fro, allowing them to travel almost instantaneously throughout the inner kingdom.

The humanoid race known as the Arianni has its origin in the Mother Constellation, Lyra. Over several millennia, various humanoid races migrated to other star clusters. Some of these original Lyran migrants found their way to the planet Earth. More recent history told the stories of the ancient civilizations of Atlantis and Lemuria.

Atlantis was the first recorded casualty of Earth human evolution. This highly technical civilization developed weapons of mass destruction while supporting a population heavily weighted with individuals at a frequency of development that honored greed, power and selfishness. The entire continent sank after the use of colossal solar powered weapons which caused a shift in the tectonic plates of the Earth's surface. As a result, a giant earthquake destroyed the Atlantian civilization. Those who survived fled to the Eastern side of the South American continent. In order to subsist, they lived in massive cave communities because the volcanic ash so polluted the atmosphere; that they could not live on the surface. Today, those subterranean survivor's progeny still occupy territory deep in the mountains of Brazil and Argentina and many have migrated through underground channels to the West Coast areas now known as Peru, Ecuador, Chile and some of the smaller territories on the northern coast of the continent.

Lemuria suffered a similar fate somewhat later as the residents of this Pacific Ocean island continent fled to areas in Southeast Asia and to the west coast of the North American continent as their eco-system began to collapse. The demise of Lemuria was linked, in part, with the disaster in Atlantis. The sinking of Atlantis interrupted the stability of Earth's fragile tectonic plates, which inevitably caused the companion sinking of Lemuria.

One of the most famous and well-known entry portals on the North American continent, Mount Shasta, is a dormant but poten-tially active volcanic mountain situated in the interior of northern California. The legendary subterranean city of *Telos* is directly under the mountain and can be reached through specific portals of entry.

The Arianni, the root race of the inner Earth, are predominantly of a Nordic stock and speak with a slightly guttural Germanic accent. They vary in height from 6' to 7' tall. Their skin is slightly tinged jade with a luminous quality, most likely because of the effects of the inner sun. Their smiles bear an uncanny resemblance to the facial structure of a dolphin's mouth. They generally feature light to blonde hair color, although not as deep a shade of blonde as commonly found on the surface of Earth. Their eyes still maintained the rounded shape from their original ancestors, but the colors are generally a soft to deep green. The ears are slightly pointed at the top with wide ear openings that contribute to their acute hearing capability. Other than those slight anomalies, the Arianni are remarkably similar to their cousins residing on the surface.

As a race, the Arianni are highly technically oriented and possess many advances unknown to the surface world, as well as unknown to most other interplanetary subterranean civilizations. They are the creators and stellar charter members of the Galactic Alliance, cooperatively formed to assure and promote lasting peace with other worlds within the Galaxy.

The Arianni are a practical and tolerant race of people – up to a certain point. Long ago they determined that the inner Earth population could only accommodate a finite number of inhabitants. Consequently, they agreed that they would limit their population through birth control systems. They instituted a policy that citizens would need to fit certain agreed-upon criteria and apply to the government for permission to have children. It was a democratic process where all citizens were given equal consideration, although there were some exceptions that the government could allow that fell outside of the criteria. The program has been highly effective and has afforded the opportunity for extensive services and essential goods to be made available to the entire population.

The *Acculturation Project*, as it was called, was adopted so as to not upset the delicate balance of their material resources in support of their spiritual natures. The foremost requirement was that any potential permanent resident would be trained in the process of becoming aware of their *total* multi-dimensional existence. The basics of *awareness* meant understanding and practicing the rapport between their third dimensional identities, such as prevails in the general population, especially on the surface world, and the simultaneous spiritual connection leading ultimately to ascension of their souls. Arianni elders wanted each member of their society to realize that the third dimensional world is only the bottom step of the spiritual ladder, limited by time and relativity, and that the higher levels are indicative of our authentic selves, not the third-dimensional life that seems to reflect everyday beliefs. The vast majority of the Arianni had over the years reached the desired enlightened state, but many others were still in the process of acquiring the full acculturation. Those chosen would, with acculturation, discover how and why they can and do exist in several dimensions of being at the same time. For example, those undergoing the process learn how to access the fifth and higher dimensions and how to function as a non-physical light body while concurrently living in a physical third dimensional body. The soul's ascension is of particular importance to the elders of the Arianni. Without the understanding and practice of the aware-ness of different realms of existence, the disciples could never truly understand the connection with their bodies, their spirit, and the historical connection to the lost continent of Mu – more commonly known as Lemuria.

The influence of this ongoing process is evident in daily life as Ariannians are often seen sitting for meditation at various times of the day. It is not uncommon to find groups of Ariannians and visitors gathered together in spiritual assemblages meditating as a group. Schools, taught by Arianni instructors and advanced disciples, were readily available to the population for instruction and practice.

The Arianni, through their acculturation process, seek to

achieve two major objectives for their civilization. They value both a balanced society with minimal conflict as well as a sustainable society, one that is designed to perpetuate itself. Building a strong balanced foundational base is thought to be the key to a long-term sustainable existence.

****

Ollie, Jackie, and Thora, while sampling light tidbits in the reception area provided for them by the Arianni, were taking in the structure and architecture of the room marveling at the crystal light emanating from within the walls and the warmth generated by an indistinct radiant heating source. They could hardly believe where they were, let alone that Garrett, Gugga, and Jared would soon be greeting them in this impressive room in this even more impressive city. Jackie remarked to the others that the room appeared to have the semblance of a library as she observed how the walls were meticulously segregated into sections and surrounded by pointed, clear crystals which she assumed had to do with obtaining access to the section's information. The walls of the room emitted a progression of muted lights which seemed to provide luminosity and warmth. The formation of the walls reflected the appearance of polished granite, but with a deeper hue and warmth than a bare structure of solid rock.

Visions of the reunion were bemusing their thoughts when suddenly Garrett appeared at the doorway, bearing a huge smile and holding out his arms to all of them. Behind him, Gugga appeared and shouted out, "I love you all! Come and hug me!" Her excited voice rang through the room revealing the same beautiful young Gugga they all remembered. She and Garrett hadn't seemed to age and their radiance filled the room. Both immediately were drawn to Thora, hugging their devoted child as if she was their only consideration.

As the family reeled in ecstatic disbelief, they rushed together and embraced as never before. A familiar face appeared behind Gugga, transfixed by the emotion-filled scene. It was Jared. Yes, Jared, their long lost son and uncle.

Jared, dressed in a form-fitting pale blue uniform, was standing next to with his arm encircling a lovely, thin, light-skinned, smiling woman, as a grinning, tall, young man of pronounced Nordic features stood next to her.

Jared embraced his mother, as Jackie erupted in happy tears. "I can't believe it's you," she cried. "Look at you, you haven't changed. You are a man now. You left us as a boy!"

"Yes," Jared replied, simultaneously sharing a warm embrace with his father. "But first I want to introduce you to my wife and son. They have been anticipating meeting you for some years now. Please meet Oula. She is Arianni, born here in the middle Earth and I have her to thank for nursing me back to health after I was shot down over North Vietnam. And this is our son, Gunnar. He is fifteen years old in Earth years . . . age is somewhat different here."

Both Jackie and Ollie were overwhelmed with tears of joy. They had arrived in a virtual paradise and now were presented the gift of their lost son and family. They truly felt blessed as they hugged their son, their newest daughter-in-law, and an Arianni-human grandson that they never dreamed they had. Garrett and Gugga were equally greeted with wild expressions of love and remembrance. It was a dream come true for everybody and they had so much more to talk about, to remember, to embrace, to express their love. It seemed impossible to capture the depth of this incredible moment.

Thora was dumbfounded that she had a young male cousin, an Arianni. She felt overjoyed and excited at the prospect of getting to know a new family member, yet she was somewhat perplexed by an eerie sense of dejà vu. She knew immediately that this young man would play a significant role in events soon to unfold. With all of her clairvoyant tendencies, she had not foreseen this scenario.

Garrett and Gugga launched into their story of arriving in Agartha, the central city within the inner Earth; their flight from Spitzbergen, flying towards the polar coordinates, and confronting the American fighter planes before being snatched out of the skies by Jared in his spinning fluegelrad.[3] The recounts made for exciting banter as Ollie and Sven related the scene enthusiastically from their remembered perspective on the ground.

Questions to Jared were fielded at a dizzying pace regarding his experience of being shot down over Hanoi and being rescued by a team of inner Earth residents as he was about to be taken prisoner by North Viet-Nam soldiers. His injuries had not been severe, yet required some immediate attention. His subsequent arrival in the middle Earth was a complete shock and surprise to him, but he quickly responded in gratitude to his rescuers by embracing their gift of freedom in order to contribute to what he later determined to be service to the Arianni, service to a cause of surface peace and preservation of life within the middle Earth.

Conversations with Oula and Gunnar were predictably awkward for the Hill family. Garrett and Gugga did well to explain to Ollie and Jackie the parameters of living with the Arianni and the meshing of Oula and Gunnar with the history, culture and background of Jared, a surface-dwelling human. Oula, a medical intuitive professional and teacher, had volunteered to assist Jared in his physical recovery from the traumatic crash as well as easing his cultural transition to life with the Arianni. They quickly connected and became a bonded couple in the eyes of the Arianni and soon begot Gunnar, an unusual mix of both Arianni and surface human.

Gunnar's addition to the society became a subject of interest to the inner Earth residents as the local culture delighted in seeing how surface and inner Earth dwellers melded as a family. As a result, Gunnar was educated fully in the ways of the Arianni, exhibiting an extraordinary intellect and powers that mirrored Arianni culture, but retaining human perspectives in social and intellectual curiosity. It was expected and anticipated by the Arianni that he would eventually accompany a group of sojourners to the surface world to assist in a planned peace project.

Sven had disappeared with his companion, Solaris, for a short time, but returned to the great hall with an invitation to dine with him and some of the spiritual initiates of Telos. After a generous allotment of time for meeting and exchanging family love and stories, the group was escorted to an adjoining room where a large circular table, replete with beautifully arranged Arianni exotic foods, was prepared for dining. As they were being guided to their seats, a group of three Arianni citizens appeared with Sven and Solaris. They were introduced as Initiates of the city of Telos, who warmly welcomed the surface dwelling guests to their middle domain. The guests sat down and enjoyed a relaxing meal while the Initiates talked from a podium about Telos and the middle Earth.

The party of five was quickly transported to a large elaborate room where they were greeted by a young Arianni ambassador who bade them in perfect English, with a slightly guttural Germanic accent, to relax and wait a few moments until their welcoming party arrived. They continued to sample the beautiful array of vegetarian food and drink consisting of unrecognizable green, yellow, and red vegetables with delectable choplets of plant-based mixtures that provided a different texture and flavor to savor while they lingered in the ornate crystal-lined room. The Arianni had long ago eschewed the eating of meat because of their connection, communication, and respect for animals. The drinks were refreshing and resembled fruit drinks from the surface. The cuisine was so well presented that, except for Sven and Solaris, the party picked at the offerings as if they were attending a special banquet at a surface brunch. There were both hot and cold foodstuffs that defied their respective olfactory systems.

"Welcome to Telos! My name is Thal and I am the Arianni Ambassador to the Earth's surface, also known as just a friend to mankind from Telos. Beside me are two of my assistants, Markos and Melanka. I hope you are comfortable and enjoyed our cultural library and its ambience while waiting. You are dining adjacent to the treasure chest of the knowledge of Agartha, accumulated over the millennia and stored in the many crystals that are available in each section. This is the place where our research begins and where we keep all the records of our discoveries, our history, and acts. There is nothing else like it in the Galaxy.

"I am pleased that your family is reunited after such a long time apart. We wanted to be sure to give you enough time to greet and share with one another before we met with you. I am here to answer any questions you may have, although I realize that you will have so many questions that they will need to be answered over a period of time. And, of course, we wanted you to join us and enjoy an Arianni meal. Be assured, however, that we will answer all of your queries. We have prepared for you living arrangements in a special area we call *The Commons*, where you will be quartered and well taken care of as our guests for as long as you wish to remain with us."

Sensing an opening for her to approach Thal, Thora respectfully, with the velvet wrapped Holy Lance in her hand, rose and stepped forward, presenting it to Thal.

"I believe this is yours," Thora quietly spoke. "I have been holding it for many years and now I have the privilege to return it to you."

Thal smiled widely as he acknowledged Thora's gift.

"Ah, my dear Thora, thank you for your diligence in protecting this holy artifact. However, it was entrusted to your keeping ever since our messenger, who your people have aptly referred to as the *Man in Black,* delivered it to you after your father and mother returned it to us. It is our wish that you keep it in your possession inasmuch as you, along with some others, are destined to utilize its power for peace on this planet. Soon, you will understand what I mean."

Thora, somewhat taken aback by Thal's pronouncement, stepped backwards as the Holy Lance was placed once again into her hands, as early childhood visions of her destiny replayed in her mind.

---

[1] Runic Triangle: This is the base unit of a portable configuration utilizing three letters of the ancient Runic Alphabet. When an energizer stone is placed in the center of the triangle, it emits an energy that allows the bearer to open seemingly locked or blocked portals.

[2] Arianni: resident population of the inner Earth.

[3] Flugelrads: Germanic expression for flying space machines, also known world-wide as Flying Saucers.

Chapter 4

THE COMMONS

*a*fter an amazing reunion with family, Ollie and Jackie were escorted to their temporary quarters some distance away. Thora remained with her parents in Agartha delighting in her reconnection with them and her uncle's family, especially Gunnar, with whom she felt an instant bond. Not knowing the Arianni customs regarding hugging, Thora could not resist throwing her arms around Gunnar. He quickly reciprocated, putting both of them as ease.

Once again, Ollie and Jackie boarded a vacuum assisted transit vehicle that whisked them away from the bowels of Agartha and deposited them at a comfortable and well-lighted relay station. Their animated conversation dwelled on the immensity of what they had just experienced as their hearts swelled with the magnitude of emotion evoked by their earlier reunion with family, intermingled with lavish commenting on the graciousness of their hosts.

They were led to a complex of housing units, known as the Commons,[1] each structure exhibiting slightly different architectural design, much like a communal village that hosted a variety of homes and shops. Their apartment was spacious and comfortable overlooking a body of water constituting an interior lake. The view of the lake seemed surrealistic to the Earth visitors as the hue projected was a combination of several colors of a spectrum.

The inner sun and its light never seemed to move. The flowing waters of the lake merged into a myriad of streams feeding into an open array of vast valleys filled with an abundance of endless vegetation. Many varieties of fruit hung in a dazzling display on an expanse of trees that stretched out for what seemed to be forever. Several large and unrecognizable animals grazed the fields, living in apparent harmony with the huge mastodons sharing the celestial atmosphere of the inner sun.

The rays of the sun reflected down upon the gigantic green forests with crystal clear running streams winding down through the surrounding mountains. Waterfalls spilled down the mountain sides emitting rainbows of golden vapors nurturing the plenitude of plant and animal life.

There was an uncanny sense of seemingly symphonic music emitting a soft somber echo throughout the valley of the sun coming from many sizes of magnificent crystalline and polished white stone buildings. Young voices arose from the many dwellings dotted along the massive warm water lakeshore. Varied shaped buildings spread for miles throughout the rolling green hills. Many of these buildings were great halls of learning occupied by hundreds of advanced, ageless, luminous beings known as the Arianni. It is said among the residents of the Commons that to drink the fresh waters and to breathe the penetrating vapors while absorbing the rays of the inner sun can sustain life forever.

The Commons itself extended out over a wide area and seemed to be able to house a large number of visitors – how many was difficult to know. Ollie and Jackie were advised that other species, aside from humans, were residents of the Commons, but all were inoffensive and well monitored by the Arianni hosts who acted as guides and information sources. All varieties of explanations were given by their hosts as to who the visitors were and why they had come. The bulk of the population consisted of short time visitors, political amnesty seekers, and invited surface humans who would become their immediate neighbors. The Colony seemed very well maintained and accommodated many other galactic species as the Arianni generously supplied the residents with all their widely diversified and perceived needs. It seemed that the Arianni fashioned their Colony much like five star hotels on the surface, complete with a number of concierges who seem to be always nearby and available.

A substantial number of the guests and residents in the Commons were quartered within neighborhood communities of similar species in order to honor comfortable familiarity. Each interplanetary species could then learn the acculturation of the inner Earth according to their varying backgrounds coupled with individual learning styles and capacities.

While Ollie and Jackie were considered to be temporary guests, they were not allowed to travel within the Hollow Earth without an escort approved by the Arianni. They were, however, given more leeway because of their relationship to Garrett and Gugga, who long ago achieved citizen status in the underground kingdom after their acculturation. As a result, Ollie and Jackie were granted the elite status of honored guests and were invited to participate in the Arianni reverse aging and healing program. Garrett and Gugga suggested to Thal that the program be granted to his parents, thinking that they might choose to stay permanently with such an intriguing initial incentive. Thal agreed to the arrangement and made ready a proposal to offer Ollie and Jackie the option of permanent residency in the inner Earth instead of choosing to return to the surface.

In fact, none of the residents of the Commons were free to travel without an escort until they had received initial training and had a basic understanding of the Arianni culture. Only those who showed the propensity for peaceful existence and willingness to adapt were allowed to visit, with escort, other parts of the underground civilization. To accomplish this orientation and training, the Arianni set up schools manned by Arianni teachers assisted by select advanced residents chosen for their sensitivity to the process.

After two days of rest and relaxation, both Ollie and Jackie were anxious to see other parts of Agartha. Garrett and Thora arrived the next day to escort the couple to a particular branch of the Agartha museum. Garrett mentioned to Ollie, as a retired naval officer, he would be especially interested in one of the exhibits. As they entered the museum, they were struck by the huge number of artifacts that they could not identify. It was apparent to the visitors that the Arianni collection of historical artifacts and antique pieces was much more sophisticated than anything they had ever seen on the surface.

As they walked into a large display room, Garrett moved towards the wall and flipped a switch. Instantly there appeared a large World War II German submarine marked U-530 perched on a sturdy platform dominating the room. It appeared to be perfectly preserved and displayed in remarkable detail.

"Do you recall the history of this U-Boat?" Garrett asked.

Ollie pondered what he was seeing in total disbelief.

"Is this the boat that the Captain sailed on to take the Spear of Destiny to Antarctica? I can't believe it is here and perfectly preserved. I was under the impression that it was scuttled in Argentina."

Garrett grinned at his dad and casually commented, "Yes, it is the U-530, but is a three-dimensional holographic image that the Arianni developed. Your recollection is correct; the boat was scuttled in Argentina. The Arianni wanted to preserve the image because it represented one of the modern journeys of the Holy Lance."

"My God," uttered Ollie," Is there anything the Arianni can't do?"

Below the impressive display on an embossed granite-like smooth stone, was the story of the U-530, its purpose, mission, list of the crewmembers, and its ultimate fate. It also chronicled the original purpose of choosing Ollie and then Garrett as the next recipient of the power of the Holy Lance.

Garrett paused to enjoy his father's expression of awe as he pondered the image. Then, he directed Ollie's attention to another part of the vast museum.

"Check this out, Dad!" Garret said, as he moved to a nearby exhibit and turned on the lights revealing the display. Ollie stared at the Tri-motor plane of Admiral Byrd, the same aircraft that Gugga and Garrett flew to the safety of the inner Earth with the Holy Lance.

"My goodness" Ollie gasped. "I suppose that this is another holographically induced image that the ever clever Arianni have created!"

"Well, there are many other images that are contained in this holographic museum. But I thought these two would be of the most interest to you. What do you think?"

"I am flabbergasted," giggled Ollie, shaking his head with a huge smile on his face. "I never would have believed this if I wasn't staring at these remarkable creations. I'm familiar with holographic art, but I never anticipated that objects could be replicated in such detail and in three dimensions. What a feat!"

"I knew you would enjoy and appreciate this display. There is so much more to the Arianni and their technology – this is just the tip of the iceberg."

Ollie was dumbstruck. Finding his name attached to a historical context in the Hollow Earth jogged his memory of how this whole chapter in his life began... his relationship with Admiral Byrd, the appearance of Thal and the flugelrad, and the debriefing by the now familiar MIBs in the States, the introduction to Sven, and other scattered details of that progression of events. This proved to be an emotional moment in time for Ollie. He realized that, after all the turmoil he witnessed, the Sacred Holy Lance was now in the hands of his granddaughter, Thora. Would this be her salvation or her demise? Tears welled up in Ollie's eyes as Jackie clutched his arm to comfort him.

****

Later that evening, after reflecting on the experiences of the day, Ollie and Jackie decided to venture out of their apartment and sample some Arianni cuisine at one of the Common's village restaurants – a unique experience, to say the least. They weren't sure exactly what it was they finally ordered, but were confident that it would be tasty and were certainly willing to try something completely new. The pleasant little restaurant was not a disappointment. Both enjoyed their respective mysterious delicacies, sharing unique tasty tidbits with one another as they giggled throughout the experience. They topped off their meal with a warm cup of a tart and fruity beverage, a fine Arianni tea that the server recommended.

It wasn't long after, with the couple lounging at their table quietly after their meal, that Ollie noticed a man who looked vaguely familiar walk into the restaurant and sit in close proximity to them. The man has to be a complete stranger, Ollie thought. Such feelings are common when one is in a strange place.

And yet, Ollie couldn't stop staring at the man, which prompted the stranger to finally rise from his chair and walk resolutely over to Ollie and Jackie's table.

"It seems as if fate has brought us together again, Commander Hill," the man spoke, extending his right hand to Ollie, inviting a handshake.

Ollie almost fell back in his chair as the recollection became clearer in his mind. It was the Captain – yes, the man who had claimed to be Gugga's long lost father who, as a member of the Teutonic Knights, had pursued him, Garrett and Gugga out of Wewelsburg Castle to the northern Norwegian town of Spitzbergen – threatening to kill them if they did not turn over the Holy Lance to him.

"I was informed you were coming," the Captain continued. "I had a meeting and conversation with both Garrett and Gugga in preparation for your arrival. I'm afraid they are still wary of me, but they have recognized the amnesty that the Arianni have granted me and have entered a period of experimental tolerance toward me, if not trust. I hope, perhaps, we can reach the same sort of accommodation."

Ollie was speechless. How in the world could this be happening? Why was this man admitted to the sanctity of the Hollow Earth? "How should I handle this?" he thought to himself, too shocked to immediately respond.

The Captain, sensing the challenge that his presence evoked, broke the awkward silence.

"This, of course, is your lovely wife," the Captain gushed. "Please allow me to re-introduce myself," he said, speaking directly to Jackie.

"My name is Otto Wermoutt, formerly a member of the German Reichsmarine, now a permanent resident of the Commons. It would please me if you would address me as Otto, if you choose. I no longer wish to be known as Captain Wermoutt. Those days are long past. I am here to start a new life."

Jackie, mostly out of habit, extended her hand to the Captain, feeling rather strange that they would meet again after the turmoil he initiated at their respective son and daughter's wedding. Memories of that day began to cloud her mind once again.

"Rather than give you a history of my transition at this time," the Captain persisted, "Perhaps we can meet again in a more comfortable and private environment so I may tell you what occurred in Wewelsburg and Spitzbergen. You don't have to concur at this moment, but perhaps, after you have had some time to reflect, I can give you a call and open a conversation. There is much more to my story than you might imagine."

Ollie finally recovered his voice, while still suspicious of this man, replying, "Perhaps I could consider your request, but not until I've had a chance to talk to Garrett and Gugga to hear their thoughts. You have a lot of explaining to do. Give me a few days and then you may call and I will give you my answer."

Wermoutt, without further adieu, excused himself and allowed his good wishes to conclude their chance meeting.

"Well," said Jackie, after Wermoutt left the restaurant, "That was a complete shock, wasn't it? He does seem sincere and very well spoken and polite though. What will you do?"

"I'm not sure. Let's wait until we talk to the kids."

With that, Ollie and Jackie retreated back to their apartment, shocked at the appearance of the Captain, now to be known as Otto, and a fellow resident of the Commons.

The next day, as planned, Garrett and Gugga journeyed to the Commons to have breakfast with Ollie and Jackie. There was still a great deal more to talk about and discuss. Garrett and Gugga had a host of questions themselves, especially how Thora had adjusted to life in Berkeley and her educational career. Ollie and Jackie brought them up to date as best they could realizing other questions would have to wait until they could spend more time together. Jackie was anxious to let Garrett know that Thora had acquired a love interest, the young man from the university named Ragnus Raggnesson. Both Garrett and Gugga were intrigued at that bit of news.

Ollie was anxious, of course, to ask his son about the Captain. He related the surprise encounter that had taken place the prior evening. He questioned Garrett about the nature of the previous meeting he had had with the Captain and asked what his understanding was of how the Captain came to be admitted to the Hollow Earth. "What was going on?" Ollie pressed Garrett in a bewildered tone.

"Well," countered Garrett, "His presence here was as much a surprise to us as I'm sure it is to you. My first reaction was one of disbelief, anger, and I suppose some fear at seeing him again."

Gugga quickly interjected, "Yes, and I still don't trust him, even though he is my father. But Thal granted him amnesty and residency here, which indicates that the Captain, as an associate of the Arianni for some years now, had succeeded in proving that he was caught up in some unfortunate circumstances. We since have adjusted to him being here and have decided to honor Thal's decision, even if we still might harbor some serious doubts and misgivings."

"Hmmm…" reflected Ollie. "I can try to comprehend that – I suppose. But I think I will accept his call as he requested. It would be interesting to hear how he has absolved himself and gained the trust of Thal."

****

It came as a surprise when Thal offered Ollie and Jackie the opportunity to take part in the age reversal and healing process. It was such a bizarre concept for them to get their heads around. Who ever thought of age reversal? What would it mean to them? With that, of course, came the invitation to permanently take up residence in the Commons and begin their own acculturation process. They were told that they could try it for awhile, but if they decided to return to the surface permanently they would face the traditional fate of growing older. But, suggested Thal, if they decided to return to Agartha after a short respite in Berkeley, they could immediately continue with the program. They, however, would need at some point to make a permanent choice because acculturation is a process that requires a strong commitment and is irreversible.

What a dilemma! Ollie and Jackie could live and grow younger in Agartha, but give up all that they were part of on the surface world; or return to the surface and resume their old life without the benefit of age reversal or healing opportunities. This would prove to be the biggest decision they had ever made, but one they vowed they would make together at the appropriate time!

****

Otto was delighted upon hearing from Ollie that he would meet him. They quickly agreed on meeting at the same restaurant where they met previously. There were enough private nooks where they would be undisturbed.

Otto greeted Ollie warmly and immediately launched into an articulate explanation and interpretation of their shared history.

"First, I want to again acknowledge that I am Gugga's father. I cannot easily excuse my earlier behavior while she was growing up. But I was essentially married to my career and made a choice. Yet I continued to send money to care for her to her grandmother. I'm not proud of my decision, but it was what it was. I would, however, in these current circumstances, like to reestablish a relationship with her. That may be difficult, but it's my fondest wish."

"That may be well and good," Ollie uttered back in a low but demanding voice, "But how do you explain your actions to bring Garrett to Germany and present some preposterous ideas to him, not to mention the frightening pursuit of us all the way to Spitzbergen?"

"Ahh, Spitzbergen..." the Captain quietly muttered, "That is where the story of my being here actually begins. Let me take us back to that day."

Otto relaxed back in his chair, looked around for any eavesdroppers and gazed deeply with his steely blue eyes directly at Ollie.

"I want to be completely honest and forthright with you. This has been a very upsetting series of revelations. Yes, I was a member of the Ancient Order of the Teutonic Knights that brought your son to Wewelsburg Castle to represent them in their quest to acquire the powers of the Holy Lance. I served the Order since the end of the war and was an integral part of their organization. They commissioned me to assist them in securing the Holy Lance in Wewelsburg Castle, while we attempted to recruit a peaceful warrior to utilize the power of the Lance. Garrett was our choice and was approved by the Arianni."

"My memory has not failed me," Wermoutt continued. "Those fateful occurrences live in my conscience and permeate my soul.

As we became stranded on the breaking ice islands, we realized that we had failed in retaining the Lance. It is my understanding that you and Sven contacted the Norwegian authorities and they sent a rescue ship to free us from a potential disaster. They arrived and took us to their headquarters for questioning. We, of course, told them very little of our actual mission, but tried to emphasize the unwanted international attention that would accompany such an inquiry. After a couple of days, they agreed to return us to Spitzbergen where we could leave in our plane while not making too much of a fuss over the incident."

"Well, we were not aware of your plight inasmuch as we got into my plane and flew off to safety," Ollie recounted.

"Unfortunately, that's where my personal troubles truly began," the Captain muttered quietly. He stopped talking for a moment, pensively recalling the entire incident. Gathering his emotions once again, he continued.

"The Knights immediately turned on me, blaming me for the failure of the mission and suggesting that I was either a traitor or not a committed patriot to the cause. I protested, but to no avail. They decided to abandon me in Spitzbergen and made it clear that I was no longer a member of their noble group. It was unbelievable! They returned to their plane and headed back to Wewelsburg Castle, their confidence somewhat shattered by the impossible turn of events.

"I thought I was doing the world a favor by bringing Garrett to them as their ambassador of peace. When Garrett flew off with the Holy Lance, I thought he was stealing it for his own benefit and led an expedition to recover it. I now know that he was trying to protect the Lance from the Knights. I was bewildered that the Knights didn't understand my actions. I felt so abandoned. I thought we were working for the same cause, but I realized that the Knights had plans to secure the Lance so they could utilize it for their own purposes. They, obviously, looked at the past holders of the Lance and, even as they realized that almost all the past holders utilized the Lance for nefarious purposes, they reasoned that they could benefit from doing the same. I didn't know that their plans were to create an immoral domain, the semblance of a fourth Reich, and the plan was that I, apparently, would be eliminated after the Lance was safely in their possession."

"Why didn't they undertake this use of power when they had the Lance in their possession at Wewelsburg? They could have used the power without all the intrigue," Ollie reasoned.

Wermoutt quickly clarified. "They believed that they needed a ruse to appease the Arianni, but when they lost the Lance to Garrett and Gugga, they decided to abandon the ruse and engage the power in the same way it had been used in the past by historic sovereigns. I am ashamed to admit that I had unwittingly played into the plot to fool the Arianni, who trusted me to enlist Garrett for what they thought would be a quest to find and recommend a surface human to hold the Holy Lance. After thorough research, and with the Arianni's input through their familiarity with you and Admiral Byrd, I had settled on Garrett as the next holder of the powers of the Lance. I thought hard on what that actually might portend; a leader who would promote world peace. Those thoughts led me to rethink and repurpose my original mission and somehow make amends with the Arianni, with the possibility of perhaps assisting you and Garrett in the mission."

"That still doesn't explain why you are *here*, here in a spiritual land of peace and tranquility," Ollie puzzled.

The Captain nodded his head at the question. "Let me explain further. While I was alone in Spitzbergen, Thal, an old acquaintance that I had many dealings with on several issues regarding the Lance and the search for a unique leader, arrived over Sven's hanger shortly after I sequestered myself. I stayed there because I had no other place to go, although I feared that the polar bear might return. I had a couple of sleepless nights there. Thal landed his fluegelrad at the airfield as he heard from his defender squadron that something was taking place of which he needed to be aware. I was so happy to see him and told him what happened. He, I believe, because of our past friendship and association, suggested I come with him to the inner Earth and invited me to stay in the Commons and begin acculturation. Of course, I immediately accepted and have taken up residence here while attending to my acculturation process.

"In addition, a few months later, Thal granted me the privilege to travel to the surface on occasion as I still have many friends and contacts there. I am able to utilize a few of the several portals that lead from the surface to the interior. I am very grateful to Thal for granting me that goodwill. I believe he knows that I can still be of useful service to the Arianni – and I intend to be.

"I want so much to atone for my foolishness and have come to realize that I should have been more aware of Garrett's intentions. We were, in point of fact, always on the same side. Thal understood that. That's why I was delighted to find you here in the Commons. You might be the bridge to my daughter. She is who I care about now."

"That's quite a story, Captain Wermoutt," sighed Ollie, "I will share it with my son and daughter-in-law. Your version of events seems plausible, but please excuse me if I choose to remain a skeptic for now. I know that Gugga will be intrigued by your story and I will leave it up to her to decide."

"Of course, Commander, I understand your position. We are, in so many ways, cut from the same cloth, as you Americans like to say. We both were faithful patriots and citizens while in our respective naval services. I certainly respect your assessment as an honorable man and officer."

---

[1] The Commons: *The Commons*, also referred to as the Colony
by the residents, acted both as a temporary way-station and
accommodations for visitors as well as permanent quarters to those
who chose to stay in the subterranean city environs. None of the
residents or visitors could travel elsewhere in the Hollow Earth
without approval or escort by an approved Arianni guide. Any
resident, however, could opt to return to the surface and would be
immediately allowed to do so. Those who stayed, however, were
encouraged to attend substantial classes that informed and taught
them the culture of the Arianni. The "culture" consisted of specific
lessons that were necessary for any surface dweller or alien to master
before she or he could be accepted in Arianni society.

The first lesson consisted of the rudiments of adjusting to the Arianni
practice of age reversal. They had, as a society, learned a spiritual
practice that gave them the power to reverse the aging process.
Consequently, even those who were quite old had the look and
physicality of a much younger individual. For some, this was a great
incentive to stay in Agartha for if they left, the aging process would
begin again.

The second lesson, and certainly the most important, was for the
individual to learn how to be aware of their authentic being, a
spiritual quest that gave the individual access to realms beyond the
third dimension. Through processes void of thinking and reasoning,
such as true meditation to achieve a state of simply being rather
than doing, residents practiced daily the art of living concurrently
in another dimension, initially the fifth dimension. This could be
a daunting task to master the process, but the Arianni knew that if
the residents stayed in the confines of time and relativity of the third
dimension, they would never adjust to the Hollow Earth culture and
enter a new state of authenticity.

Chapter 5

MOLEA AND THE ANNUNAKI

*L*ord Molea, the Sovereign of the Annunaki, shifted uneasily in his chair as he was confronted with the painful dilemma of what to do to save his people.

The Annunaki, a reptilian bi-pedal species native to Venus, had retreated to the center of the planet eons ago as the surface became uninhabitable. The Annunaki were forced to seek refuge in the subterranean realm of inner Venus, where they reestablished their civilization. The populace managed to thrive and prosper in their underground kingdom as they were able to continue to withdraw nitrogen from the outer atmosphere as the surface steadily deteriorated. Nitrogen in gaseous form is essential to the existence of the Annunaki, just as oxygen is critical to maintaining life for the inhabitants of planet Earth. Nitrogen is not only necessary for respiration, but provides nourishment as a form of "food" to sustain the bodies of the Annunaki.

An innovative and pragmatic species, the Annunaki determined the number of people that could be supported in their inner colony. Out of necessity, they began to regulate their reproduction in order to maintain a steady population size that could be sustained with the limited amount of nitrogen they had storehoused.

Over the last century, however, a devastating climate change had been underway, causing nitrogen depletion in the inner atmosphere that threatened to destabilize the habitation and make it unsuitable for maintaining life. Over the years, the Annunaki leaders had explored many potential mitigations to their nitrogen issue, including manufacturing nitrogen through chemical and mechanical means. To date, none of the possible solutions explored had achieved significant results. Alternative production processes had been ineffective in producing or enhancing the nitrogen content to the degree necessary to meet the needs of a static population numbering nearly a half million beings, half the size of the population of the Hollow Earth. The situation was becoming critical with more and more outbreaks of illness and reports of death in certain sectors. The pressure for an immediate solution was mounting, and the mood in the Annunaki interior world was approaching desperation.

He glanced over at his daughter, Lady Roola, and uttered, "I am at a loss to know what to do. Every choice seems to be a death wish for us."

****

The Annunaki are a reptilian race of humanoids created by the scientific experimentations of the Vegans, from the star system Vega, a civilization that split from the constellation Lyra, the mother constellation of all humanoids. They became a viable group of self-sustaining bipedal humanoids by the gene-splicing proclivities of Vegan scientists. The Vegans confined their gene experiments to reptiles inasmuch as they were the only other species either known or available to the Vegans. The Annunaki developed physical traits of humans combined with striking reptilian features that were not anticipated by the Vegans. The newly created humanoid species joined with the other fragmented humans who left Lyra and settled in other constellations such as Apex, Sirius, the Pleiades, Orion, Arcturus, and the planet now known as Venus.[1]

Physically, the Annunaki closely resemble a bi-pedal human with the overriding characteristics of a reptilian species. They stand nearly six foot in height with slightly oval and protruding heads, somewhat resembling a legendary dragon, featuring protruding red eyes highlighted by yellow vertical pupils. Their close-cropped ears and lipless green mouths hide much smaller teeth and a lack of incisors characteristic of humans. The complete outer skin consists of a number of green/black solid smooth scales that measure, when an adult, from one half to three inches in length, depending on the body part. Their heads and arms exhibit the smallest scales.

The Annunaki have two long and flexible jointed arms, with a narrow set of elongated hands somewhat larger than that of a human. Their hands are fitted with three flexible fingers with an opposing flat thumb-like appendage. The legs and feet are similar to the composition of their arms and hands with flexible pointed toes. They are able to move effortlessly while in a human form, much like human beings, and are active with their extremities. Although hampered by some structural limitations, such as torso flexibility, they possess keen eyesight, acute hearing, and an adaptable command of alien speech – common characteristics of the Annunaki that help them to communicate their understanding by use of diverse sounds and languages.

In confronting the prospect of the extinction of their race, the leaders had begun to explore the possibility of migrating to a planet with an atmosphere that could sustain their population. The Annunaki had noted that the atmosphere of the Earth contained nearly 80% nitrogen on the planet's surface. More than ten years ago, they had begun infiltrating the Earth's surface by sending pioneer emissaries to explore the potential for a more extensive Annunaki colonization of the blue planet.

The Annunaki were, of course, aware of the extensive population on the Earth's surface, but believed they could potentially infiltrate the species using their ability as *shape-shifters*. Using a holographic image which they could project into human minds, they were able to assume a human or other form for over a few days before having to recharge their status. It was a process that only took a few moments to accomplish and was more of a nuisance than a problem. The only issue was to keep their reptilian figure in a human form so as not to alarm the surface population. Over the last few years, some progress had been made. They targeted a relatively unoccupied area of North Asia to set up an experimental settlement. The Annunaki had effectively populated some especially remote and beleaguered regions of the Earth where they were able to influence some of the more unsophisticated Earth dwellers to accept and even cooperate with them, inciting mistrust and conflict among the residents where it served their purposes.

However, the Annunaki were wary of the inner dwellers of their companion planet. The Arianni, whose technological advances were thought to be more advanced than those of their own, could pose a serious threat should they initiate a mass evacuation to the blue planet.

The Arianni, after fighting a reluctant but successful war against the Annunaki eons ago, seemed to have little interest in the meager activities of the Annunaki on the surface of Earth as they deemed there was no imminent threat to them. Since that ancient war, both interior populations had settled into isolated colonies quite disassociated from one another. The only contact was through the Galactic Alliance, an informal advisory body for inner planets. The Alliance met only when approached by a member planet because of a potential major conflict with another civilization. There had been peace for a millennium, with the Arianni seemingly allowing unconcerned passive consent to the Annunaki's more recent presence on relatively unpopulated areas on the surface of the Earth.

The Annunaki hoped the Arianni would continue to take a passive path and stay in their fortressed interior without contesting their recent activity. The Annunaki could not accurately predict, however, whether or not the Arianni, a historically non-aggressive people, would attempt to prevent them from their colonization quest.

They were aware that the Arianni protective squadron, a fully armed flugelrad fleet that varied in active numbers between four and ten, continually monitored the Earth surface to assure that nothing occurring on the surface would disrupt the peace and continuity of the inner Earth. Not only did the Arianni have enlightened concerns about the surface human population's use of atomic weapons and their propensity for violence, they were alert to the subtle incursion of the Annunaki and keeping close watch on their activities.

****

Roola had long been Molea's closest confidant, with their relationship continuing to deepen as she grew older. An only child, Roola's wisdom was unusual for someone so young, yet Molea sought her input constantly. He gazed lovingly at his daughter now, who had retained her mother's predominance of human rather than reptilian features. The influence of the reptilian traits varied among the population, with some retaining more human DNA than others. Roola's mother, who died in childbirth, had exhibited substantially more human physical characteristics, which were passed on to Roola. This more human appearance opened the way for a potential relationship between Roola, of the Annunaki, and other humanoid species. By Annunaki standards, Roola was considered attractive even as she only displayed minimal reptilian physical traits. All were aware that Roola was the heir apparent to Molea's sovereign leadership.

As a sovereign leader, Molea had proven himself over time to be both wise and reflective. It was he who had met with Thal, a leader of the Arianni, several Earth years ago to forge an agreement for limited residency on Earth until they found a nitrogen depletion solution. His scientists, however, had been stumped at each potential breakthrough, only discovering a partial solution to its nitrogen depletion. His lieutenants were restless and there was heated talk of rebellion in the ranks to actively force Molea to ramp up the evacuation plan.

Molea was becoming more and more isolated in his position and under continual pressure to implement immediate and large scale evacuation to the Earth surface.

Roola, in her sincere desire to assist her father in making this momentous decision, suggested, "Why don't you call a special sitting with Thal of the Arianni and explain our dilemma? He has no reason to reject you and I'm sure he would confer with you on a host of possible solutions without us needlessly alienating him by simply approving an evacuation without his knowledge or consent."

Molea pondered on his daughter's sage advice. He was always very proud of his highly educated and intelligent daughter, and after a protracted pause, said, "Well, that would be a temporary respite, but the inevitability of evacuation would alert Thal to a potential threat. The inner Earth society might take measures to thwart us."

"Evacuation is not necessarily inevitable – perhaps Thal and the Arianni have developed technology that could help us," retorted Roola. "Knowing the alternatives and the desperate dilemma we are in would surely trigger his support. Isn't it worth a try?"

Goran and Plotus entered the leader's chamber intending to persuade and encourage Molea to begin the evacuation immediately. Goran, the chief military and personal advisor to Molea, had been viewed as the second in command for many decades. His advice to Molea had been practical and effective on many occasions. Molea, was nevertheless concerned that Goran sometimes acted before thinking through the intended and unintended consequences of all the available options. Goran, at this point, believed evacuation and relocation to be the only viable course of action. He wasn't convinced that the Arianni would challenge them, and his view was to take action and deal with the Arianni in the future if the need arose.

Goran's aggressive tone pounced on the apparent indecision of the Annunaki leader as he bellowed, "We are running out of time, dear leader. We must act now!"

Goran's companion, Plotus, himself a trusted and long-time advisor in domestic affairs, followed Goran's plea with an impassioned appeal of his own.

"Surely, dear leader, there is no alternative. We must prepare for evacuation. Continuation of our civilization depends on it!"

Molea was struck by the thunderous assertiveness of his advisors, especially Plotus, who had always been the most reserved and thoughtful of his lieutenants. Molea arose and began pacing around the table where he had been seated, staring with helpless eyes at his daughter while glancing back at the troubled faces of his lieutenants.

"I hear you, dear advisors, and I will undertake a mass evacuation if necessary as a last resort. But first I am going to follow the suggestion of Roola to arrange a meeting with Thal and the Arianni on Earth. I want to avoid any misunderstanding that might lead to conflict. It would be imprudent for us to save our civilization only to face a war with a powerful adversary that could potentially overwhelm us."

Goran's face turned ashen. He stood for a moment in disbelief at his leader's hesitance and turned to Plotus, whose face had a look of apprehension.

"Yes, dear leader, that sounds like a good plan," Goran sardonically replied. "When will you leave?"

Molea, somewhat relieved at the neutral sounding response from Goran, replied, "Well, as soon as possible – perhaps tomorrow."

With the response from Molea that they had anticipated, Goran and Plotus glanced at one another furtively, acknowledged the sovereignty of their leader with a bow, and exited the room.

Roola quickly offered to help her father make arrangements to travel to Earth, saying she would contact Thal on his behalf to assure an audience for the two of them. Molea felt desperate and wanted to make the connection as soon as possible. He encouraged Roola to act at once.

Within a short period of time, Molea was on his way to Earth. Roola had secured the invitation from the Arianni leader and travelled with him. Molea was received in the crystal city of Agartha, the capital of the Arianni civilization in the shape-shifting form of a human. Because Roola embodied many of the physical characteristics of humans, she did not feel the need to shape shift. A special entrance vortex was created by the Arianni to allow Molea and Roola to enter the center of the Earth. They were then escorted to the Great Hall of Asgarth, where previous meetings between the two civilizations had taken place over the millennia.

****

As Goran and Plotus left the quarters of Molea, Goran grasped Plotus firmly by the arm and whispered to him passionately, "This is our opportunity. While he is gone we will assume power and not allow Molea to return to this planet. We will take the necessary steps to evacuate the planet and prepare for a potential war with the Arianni. It is our duty to do this. Our planet will not survive and we must save our people now. It is a risk we must take. We must do this! "

Plotus nodded his head in reluctant agreement. Until this moment, he had always followed the direction of Molea, but now, with Goran's fearful but compelling logic, he agreed that desperate measures had to be taken.

He asked Goran, "Don't we have a disadvantage knowing the superior technology of the Arianni?"

Goran looked at him with some distain. "Plotus," he said, "There are many ways to conduct a war. I am not so foolish to simply challenge the obvious strength of the Arianni."

A mischievous smile accompanied Goran's words. Plotus could only guess what might be lurking in Goran's intentions. He would, he decided, work with Goran to begin preparations for evacuation and possible war, because he could not see a reasonable alternative. But he would remain cautious.

****

As Molea and Roola arrived in Agartha, their spacecraft entered the special vortex created specifically for them by the Arianni. The reptilian couple entered the waiting magnetic-vacuum transporter and were whisked away to meet Thal. As they entered Thal's discussion chamber, the host greeted them enthusiastically as he was accustomed to welcome guests with warmth and friendliness. The Arianni were traditionally a peaceful people and continuously welcomed travelers from other inner planets.

Molea, not one to delay his message with time-wasting salutations, immediately began to tell Thal of his predicament with the nitrogen depletion and the potential of evacuation. His plea was received compassionately by Thal as he empathized with his fellow inner planetary leader. Thal asked what he could do to help

Molea spoke with grave concern and asked Thal, "Do the Arianni have any technology that could assist us in nitrogen generation or re-generation?"

Thal answered directly and forthrightly. "I'm afraid not, at least not now, but we will earnestly assist you in seeking a long term solution to the nitrogen issue. We have never felt the need to explore such technology due to the rich content of nitrogen that is present here."

"Well, as you know," Molea said somewhat sheepishly, "We have had some of our species on your surface to test whether Earth's surface could sustain some of our population. It's been going on for some time. Would you be open to a settlement of Annunaki in some remote unoccupied surface lands? I realize what I am asking and the effect it would have on the surface human population, but our options are limited."

"Yes, we are aware of the limited population of your people that has established itself on the Earth's surface. We have not responded because up until recently they have not caused a problem, and because of your holographic shape-shifting, the surface dwellers have not encountered major problems with your people. We do have some concern about your holographic ruse as shapeshifters when and if the human surface dwellers realize that they have been misled as to who their trusted neighbors truly are.

"I need to meet with our Supreme Council to see how they would react to an evacuation of your inner world and settlement on our surface. But I should warn you that they have been concerned about some of your holographic residents that have been infiltrating surface institutions and regions and causing some unrest among the Earth's population. That cannot be tolerated."

"I understand completely," responded Molea, "I can arrange to have my special cadre Enforcement Unit come to Earth to mitigate any concerns that you or your Supreme Council may have and/or to neutralize those who are causing such havoc."

"I will do my best to present your thoughts to the Council," replied Thal. "I will arrange a meeting with them immediately as I am sure you will need to get back to your home planet as soon as possible. We will see if the Council is open to developing a proposal to assist. Thank you for coming to alert us."

****

As Thal entered the Agarthian Great Crystal Hall to meet with the Supreme Council, he had already transmitted his conversation with Molea to the Council by telepathic communication. Meeting with the ten Supreme Council Members, however, required a physical presence as the Council would need to discuss openly the tenets of any agreement.

"And so, Great Council Members, are we able to address Lord Molea's proposal?" said Thal as he addressed the Council members.

Adama, who is the head rotating council member representing Telos, the crystal city underneath the volcanic mountain of Shasta, responded directly to Thal.

"We have a proposal," Adama replied. "I will read it to you.

"First, we are pleased to assist the Annunaki in researching and developing a nitrogen regenerator and have already set that research in motion. We will concurrently address the gradual interior and exterior warming of both planets.

"Secondly, we insist that Molea immediately take the necessary steps to remove those Annunaki that are disrupting the surface world until the research and production can be completed and implemented. If Molea is not able to eliminate the disrupters of the surface world, we will reassess our commitment to assist and take necessary measures.

"Thirdly, we will prepare to vigorously repel any uninvited colonizers coming from the Annunaki world if these conditions cannot be met. In addition, we will provide assistance to the surface dwellers of Earth to purge any Annunaki who remain or choose not to follow Molea's directives.

"Fourth, we will approach the surface world and allow them to participate in any decisions relating to evacuation and permanent settlement on the surface. We will discuss with them the possibility of relocating Annunaki on Earth's surface land that is not populated by humans.

"Lastly, we thank Lord Molea of the Annunaki for approaching us before undertaking any covert action that could instigate an interplanetary war."

"Thank you, Supreme Council," Thal replied in respect. "I will inform Molea of your decision."

Thal, with a respectful bow, exited the Supreme Council chamber and immediately made arrangements for Molea to meet with him to relay the decision of the Council.

Molea listened carefully to Thal and pondered his options. Knowing how limited his choices were, he unwaveringly accepted the terms of the Council, grateful that the Council would even consider a peaceful Annunaki evacuation and settlement on unoccupied Earth surface land. He also was delighted that the technically savvy Arianni would devote resources to developing a nitrogen generator when the Annunaki had spent decades in research and development with no result. With this provision alone, Molea felt a glimmer of hope that an evacuation and significant Earth settlement would not be necessary. He was ready to return to his home and implement the plan. He had some doubts that Goran and Plotus would readily accept this agreement, but felt confident that he had found an alternative to avert his homeland's demise.

Upon arriving back at his transporter, he was met by a host of Arianni guards who informed him that his home planet had rejected his return. Molea was nonplussed by the news. He had been ousted from his position of leader by Goran. He never considered that possibility could happen. He and Roola were now trapped on Earth.

Thal, upon hearing the news, immediately contacted Molea and offered temporary asylum within the inner Earth until the coup was either overturned or the Annunaki accepted him back as leader. He and Roola were invited to reside in The Commons where guests and travelers were billeted.

The Arianni now realized that they faced a threat from the inner culture of Venus and began preparations for defense. According to Molea, Goran would be preparing to evacuate the entire Venetian interior to settlement on Earth as soon as practical and would prepare to fight a war against the Arianni and the human surface population if either or both chose to stop them. Thal began to envision a conflict that the peace-loving Arianni could be reluctant to fight.

****

Goran planned to evacuate Venus as soon as he could arrange the logistics, and was assured that his military was prepared. With the able assistance of Plotus, who enjoyed a great deal of respect among the military leaders and the Annunaki population, Goran pressed for a contingent of warriors to be deployed as an elite advance guard to test and weaken resistance of both the surface population and the Arianni. They would make contact with the current Annunaki colonists to forge an armed alliance that would preempt any major resistance to settlement and temper any opposition to Goran's plan. The advance guard would organize an initial defense that would disrupt any perceived refusal to comply.

"We have no choice," muttered Goran, assuming the title of Lord Goran. "The survival of our species is at stake."

---

[1] Much cosmic folklore has followed the reptilian species since its inception. The history of these bipedal humanoids indicate that they have been typically shunned and feared throughout the Galaxy. They have been chronicled by some to be invaders utilizing their shape-shifting ability and have assumed the form of Earth surface leaders who favored igniting the war like passions of the surface population in order to turn them against one another and assure the dominance of the Annunaki. It is asserted that many of the autocratic leaders, as well as some populist leaders of Earth, are Annunaki. They are known as the original shapeshifters.

Chapter 6

THE CLASH

*T*he pioneer contingent of Annunaki, already solidifying their presence on the surface of Earth, felt very secure in their occupation of the remote, sparsely populated, Earth territory north of the Asian Sub-Continent. They had been resident-visitors of Earth for over 25 years and led a quiet existence within the confines of the territory. The territory was considered a 'banana belt" as it defied the inclement climatic conditions predominant in the region.

The Annunaki, in their shapeshifted human form, appealed to the natural fears of the Earth dwellers and worked through another dimension where they blended in holographically with human bodies. They correctly assumed that taking on human form rather than exhibiting their natural reptilian appearance would obviate any issues arising from the radical difference of appearance between the two species. They also learned that Earthlings were vulnerable to fear and began to organize them in pursuit of change that would benefit the Annunaki.

The Annunaki had stealthfully modified the Earth's local environment to suit their needs, hopeful not to alienate or disturb the relatively few humans residing in the area. They had gradually shared a bit of their advanced technology to convince the local human surface dwellers that they were becoming neighbors with a great deal to offer the remote population of humans. They were able to supply the Earth dwellers with wireless electricity and certain agricultural techniques adapted for generally harsh climatic conditions, which were much appreciated by the population. The Annunaki residents were gradually accepted into the territory and were even elected to positions of leadership by the unaware, yet grateful human residents. As such, the Annunaki had come to assume some leaderhip within the area where they began to shape the social and physical environment to their advantage.

The human population had been amazed at the expertise these people had brought to make their arid landscape arable. For many years, blind appreciation salved any suspicion toward the new residents and their presence was uniformly welcomed. But over time, some friction had begun to arise between the Annunaki and their human neighbors as rumors began to circulate. The disguised Annunaki-humans in leadership positions had gradually begun to exert a more heavy-handed and authoritarian style of management over their co-residents. Concurrently, because the Venetian visitors could not hold their holographic human shapes for more than a few days before needing a "recharge," some humans thought they had caught a glimpse of something very odd taking place. That a confrontation would erupt at some point was inevitable..

The first breech in the relatively stable situation occurred when an Annunaki resident with physical transformation in progress was witnessed by a small group of local humans. As rumors of the bizarre scene spread among the human population, fear and reticence crept into the humans as they began to realize that their neighbors were not who – or what – they had been led to believe. A distrust of leadership, which had become overwhelmingly Annunaki, began to arise, causing a great deal of anxiety in the populace. As the rumors spread and fear grew, some of the local population began to meet in secret to devise ways of exposing the Annunaki.

Two of the younger surface residents of the area, Lin Sing and Mao Chu, called a group together to form a plan to expose the newly discovered anomalies. Both men, in their early twenties, were consumed with the suspicion that they were the victims of a major hoax. Lin Sing, the more aggressive of the two, convinced his long time friend and neighbor, Mao Chu, that it was up to them to take covert action on behalf of the villagers to expose the rumored deception.

Fear of the unknown, fear of the imposing actual Annunaki reptilian form and the perpetuation of the peculiar rumors, fueled both young men to action. Their plan was to simply expose the Venetian interlopers and drive them out of their land. They had no idea of the superior power of the reptilian population.

Lin Sing and Mao Chu's hastily developed plan revolved around kidnapping one of the Annunaki and retaining him captive until he was forced to reveal his true form, exposing the alien race as invaders to the rest of the populace. They believed that after the interlopers were exposed, governments of the Earth would collectively band together to eliminate the intruders of mankind.

Lin Sing and Mao Chu conspired to kidnap a local leader, who they deduced was a reptilian in disguise, and bring him back to a now growing contingency of like-minded humans in a secure encampment. Here they would extract the truth and expose the hostile infiltration and occupation of their lands by aliens.

The kidnapping was poorly planned and bungled in its execution. In the midst of the potential kidnapping, Lin Sing pulled out a sword in an attempt to coerce the victim into surrendering. In his nervous haste, he accidently sliced the arm of the kidnapped man with his weapon and, in turn, the outcry of the victim alerted other protective guards. They attacked Lin Sing, killing him instantly with a quiet laser weapon. Mao Chu retreated rapidly, running out the door, barely eluding several other Annunaki guards who were not in that moment protected by a human holographic image. The first blows of confrontation had been struck.

Colleagues and neighbors of both young men were astounded by the turn of events. A panic set in when Mao Chu told them of his encounter and the fact that he had eluded guards who were not disguised by their holographic shell.

The local townspeople banded together, gathered their outmoded weapons, and combined their resources for a revenge attack. However, they were no match for the Annunaki, who utilized their much superior weaponry to quickly suppress the disorganized uprising. A number of the gathered townspeople were killed and the Annunaki rallied to eliminate or capture any remaining survivors. The Annunaki determined that the Earth's greater population must never know of this incident. The Annunaki leaders undertook to block any information exchange and skillfully covered up the incident.

Goran, the coup leader of the Venetian Annunaki, received word of the lethal confrontation soon after the occurrence. He dispatched his special elite guards to enter the region and calm down the reptilian warrior base. He was concerned that even if the confrontation was covered up from human knowledge, the Arianni would know of it through the reconaissance provided by the Arianni overhead patrols. He recognized the incident as a serious threat to his plans of evacuation and settlement.

The elite guard of the Annunaki consisted of fifty loyal, well trained, and disciplined reptilian troops who were sent immediately to the occupied region to assure that the news of the incident would never reach any other of Earth's inhabitants. They were trained and instructed to use whatever force or coercion that was necessary to avert the spread of news or information. They arrived with orders to purge any being that threatened to divulge the knowledge of the Annunaki presence.

Muchin was anointed to be the captain of the elite guard. He was the younger brother of Goran and, as such, had the complete trust of his older sibling. He could be ruthless when needed and diplomatic as the occasion necessitated. In this case, the response could be ruthless given the gravity of the mission.

****

The Arianni overhead patrols, who were constantly monitoring the region, detected the disturbance and immediately alerted the inner Earth inhabitants that a new threat was emerging. A team was discharged from the inner Earth consisting of Garrett, Thora, and Gunnar with the directive to clandestinely meet with Mao Chu and the residents. The group arrived in their saucer-shaped craft near a remote village and quickly organized a meeting with the human leaders and their immediate neighbors. The dispirited and defeated villagers gathered in a make-shift meeting room to discuss what to do next. The villagers had lost a number of neighbors in their first attempt to expose the Annunaki as reptilians. They had no idea that the reptilians had such advanced weaponry.

Thora was the first to speak. "I know how frightened you all are. The reptilians, known as the Annunaki, have overstepped their welcome here on the surface of the Earth. They have been living here for some time, sheltered from your reality by their ability to shape-shift. They can appear as humans for a set period of time and then they must recharge in order to reassume their human appearance. You caught them in the act of shifting.

"I won't lie to you. They are dangerous and unpredictable and I beg you not to confront them again by yourselves. However, I must also tell you that you have allies throughout the Galaxy – other humanoids who will assist and help you through this crisis."

"What do you mean, throughout the Galaxy? What in the world are you talking about?" asked Mao Chu, shocked and puzzled.

"We live in a populated Galaxy. There are a number of civilizations with concerns about the activities of the Annunaki. You are not alone. I know this may be hard for you to believe, but I promise you, it is true. When you look up at the millions of stars and planets in the heavens, please understand that there are folks living there just as you live here."

The villagers were stunned to hear Thora talk. They had never truly considered that they were surrounded by Galactic civilizations that were interested in what happened on Earth. It took some new thinking for them to begin to understand the gravity of their position and face the new challenges to their belief system.

"And that's not all," continued Garrett. "There is a civilization within the center of the Earth populated by a pleasant race of humanoids that also descended from the stars. They, however, are not to be feared as they have watched over and protected the surface world for many years. They wish to help you in your plight with the Annunaki. In fact, Gunnar here is a resident of the inner Earth and is known as an Arianni."

Gunnar interrupted, "We ask only one thing from you. Do not share this information with other villages or acquaintances. We, the Arianni, will help you but we don't want to alert the general world population and send the surface world into a needless panic. Can we depend on your assistance? The Arianni have technology far beyond what you have witnessed and we have the support of the Galactic Alliance, a confederation of many companion civilizations. We all want to help. We simply need your cooperation."

The villagers, still in shock at what they just heard, all nodded their heads in agreement while still processing new realities that demanded a restructuring of their view of themselves and the cosmos.

"We, of course, will cooperate," said Mao Chu who had emerged as leader and spokesman of the stunned villagers. "We are willing to help in any way possible. And we thank you for attending here tonight and trusting us with the facts as you know them. We are very grateful for your assistance."

"To confirm who we are," said Gunnar, "We will land one of our spacecrafts nearby for you to see. I'm sure that will erase any lingering doubts."

Jared's flugelrad suddenly circled overhead the village and landed, taking Garrett, Thora, and Gunnar quickly away. The villagers once again were stunned at the sight of the spacecraft. Their lives had been altered completely.

****

Garrett's older brother, Jared, was one of the captains of the Arianni Defender's Surface Patrol (ADSP). The employ of his spacecraft allowed him to monitor the Earth surface with highly advanced technological surveillance apparatus. The stealth and speed of his craft prevented the surface dwellers from detecting his presence. Earth dwellers were unaware that the ADSP was constantly monitoring the activities of all of Earth's happenings and, in addition, they had no idea of the presence of the Annunaki colony on the Asian Sub-Continent. Only a select few groups or individuals were aware that that Arianni were residing in the center of the Earth. One of those groups, however, was the Royal Order of the Teutonic Knights, and of course Captain Otto Wermhoutt, who had worked with the Arianni to identify a holder for the Holy Lance.

Jared had reported the unusual activity to Thal, who immediately called the Arianni General Council together to reveal the alleged aggressive actions of the Annunaki. The Arianni, of course, already were aware of the twenty-five years of Annunaki colonization and had up until this point been content to observe and refrain from confrontation as violence was not an arm of their diplomacy and the Annunaki colonization was minimal.

"I believe it is time for us to introduce intercession measures to thwart any further violence," said Thal, "and to make the Annunaki aware that the Arianni will not sit by and let the Venetian colonists assume control over any of the surface dwellers' communities or their territory.

"I propose to send a small cadre of trained personnel to confront the elite guard of the Annunaki on Earth and remind them of our long-standing agreement of non-interference towards the surface dwelling population. This may be a good time to send a contingent headed by Thora and Garrett who have now been trained to harness the power and protection of the Holy Lance. We will engage through diplomacy and attempt to resolve the issue without further bloodshed. It will be a small group consisting of Garrett, Thora, and a few of their closest associates or family. Along with them, Roola, Molea's daughter, will serve as a consultant on Annunaki tactics and act as a potential liaison between the Arianni representatives and the Annunaki. Garrett and Thora will be protected by the power of the Lance. I ask your approval for this limited response."

"Thank you for the report. Please relay our support and good wishes for their success," the council president, Adama, retorted to Thal. "We would like to resolve this issue without invoking the ire of the Annunaki and increasing the tension with the traditional surface dwellers. You have our conditional approval. We ask you to proceed with restraint."

Thal, before naming his cadre, sought out Molea to inform him of the new situation. Molea covered his head in distress and apologized to Thal. He had not foreseen this turn of events leading to violent confrontations. His apology was sincere, as the intention of the meeting had been to circumvent any possible violence. However, Thal moved quickly to form the intercession group and contacted Thora and Garrett to help choose assistants for their, hopefully, diplomatic contact with the Annunaki elite guard. They settled on a small group of five Arianni warriors and patrol observers, led by Thora, Garrett, Roola, and Gunnar, the Arianni/human offspring cousin of Thora. Jared would transport them all in his craft to a nearby location where the earlier confrontation took place.

Thora and Garrett held the secrets to the Holy Lance, and its power would protect them from imminent danger from Annunaki weapons. They had spent over three months in intensive training in communication, tactics, diplomacy, and defense.

Before embarking on the mission, Gunnar would be equipped with the newly designed but marginally tested holographic instrument imprinted inlay, simply known as the Utility Arm that was embossed on his left appendage. The inlay would be activated as a communication device – to translate or communicate with either animals or alien species. It included an invisibility shield, a biologically activated switch producing an electromagnetic protective shield that renders the individual bearer temporarily invisible and impervious to attacks by others. It also had an experimental body de-materialism option to escape potential capture or harm – giving the bearer an ability to de-construct his or her body in their immediate surroundings and rematerialize it in a predetermined location. This was designed as a last resort option if other options failed. Finally, the imprinted device featured a stun instrument that rendered any aggressor temporarily helpless if used, but was not fatal unless adjusted accordingly.

The other members of the intervention team, however, could be potentially exposed to harm from the Annunaki elite guard. The goal of the strategy was that Garrett and Thora would take decisive action that would keep their companions out of harm's way and avert a possible explosion of violence.

The small Arianni contingent, led by Garrett and Thora, was landed near the site of the recent skirmish. After undertaking a surveillance of the area, preparations were made to contact the Annunaki in the area and initiate negotiations. Protected by the inherent power of the Holy Lance, Thora led Gunnar, who was equipped with the holographically embedded Utility Arm, and accompanied by Roola, to meet with the Annunaki and open negotiations to avoid further violence. Garrett remained behind with the five well-armed Arianni soldiers to act as a backup if negotiations went astray.

Thora sent an electronic message to Muchin who agreed to meet with the three in a designated location where they would not be disturbed. While Muchin seemed cooperative initially, he quickly acted upon the situation by letting Thora know that he had Earthling hostages who would be eliminated if the Arianni group threatened them in any way. Thora, nonetheless, continued to present the directives of the Arianni to the Annunaki. The Arianni directive commanded the Annunaki to return to Venus within three days, to release the local hostages allowing them to work out their own problems, and to let Molea and the Arianni negotiate a permanent and peaceful solution. Thora purposely left out any reference to Molea being overthrown by Muchin's brother.

Roola stepped forward to assist, thinking as an Annunaki she would be able to alleviate the crescendoing circumstance, but was immediately seized as an Annunaki traitor. Gunnar quickly came to Roola's defense, but he also was seized as a cadre of Muchin's soldiers appeared to reinforce their position. Holding two of the negotiators hostage gave Muchin the audacity to confront Thora with a corresponding threat. Muchin directed Thora to either leave the area immediately or all the hostages, including Gunnar and Roola, would be killed.

Thora barked back to the Annunaki commander that if any of the hostages were harmed, they would be facing an interplanetary war. She knew she could override the threat and would be protected by the power of the Lance, but she backed away from the confrontation knowing any overt action by her could put the hostages in a dangerous, perhaps fatal, situation. Her thoughts were guided by the Arianni strategy to not enflame the situation and to avoid any further loss of life, including that of the Annunaki.

Thora was anguished that she had put her cousin Gunnar and Roola in such a delicate situation. Her first inclination to react was mitigated by her inner guidance to let Garrett and Jared know the latest situation and to seek their recommendations as to what to do next.

Garrett could hardly contain his emotions upon finding out what had occurred. His daughter and Arianni nephew had been tricked by the Annunaki, and his first thought was immediate retaliation, rescue, and revenge. When Jared arrived to retrieve the group and learned of the dilemma, the concern for his son was palpable. The brothers felt that they could not just stand by and let this alien incursion threaten the lives of their beloved family members. It gave them some solace to know that Gunnar was protected by the power of the Utility Arm – but of course Roola was not.

Both, however, were restrained by the message from Thal, who was in constant communication with Garrett and Jared, urging them to refrain from any provocation until the Arianni leadership had a chance to evaluate the state of affairs. The men reluctantly agreed and returned to Agartha to confer with Thal on the best way to bring a peaceful resolution of the situation.

****

Goran immediately transported Roola back to Venus and imprisoned her for treasonous activity. He did not want her staying on Earth to possibly be released or escape. She could be used as a hostage if the need arose. Her captivity could deter any mission to overthrow his new regime and reinstate Molea. He knew, however, that word of Roola's abduction and imprisonment would awaken the ire of many Annunaki. The populace had witnessed the princess grow up next to Molea and developed a fondness for her as the *crown princess*, destined to become the sovereign after Molea's passing. He admonished his guards to maintaince secrecy around her capture and imprisonment. He feared that he could be facing a counter-coup himself if the truth got out.

Chapter 7

THE ARIANNI RESPOND

*a*t the order of Goran, Muchin sent two of his fifty warriors to accompany Roola as she was transported back to Venus to be imprisoned. As threatened, Goran deposited her in a bare cell and sealed her off from any contact with potential sympathizers. The news of her arrest and captivity was sure to cause unrest among some of the Annunaki population, so Goran sought to keep her imprisonment hushed. He felt that he could use Roola as a future bargaining chip if any overt uprising should occur.

Gunnar was left imprisoned in a hollowed out cave protected by a magnetic electronic barrier. With his Utility Arm, he knew he could escape without delay, but chose to stay to protect Roola. The two of them had begun to develop a personal trusting relationship while charged with working together toward a common purpose. As their connection was just beginning to spark, Roola was almost immediately escorted out of the cave, loaded on an Annunaki space craft and spirited off to Venus.

Gunnar decided to stay in apparent captivity so he could find out about any Annunaki plans. His Utility Arm's communication capability allowed him to know the activities of Jared and Garrett. When he was sure that they had landed nearby, he made his exit by bringing into play the invisibility shield while neutralizing the electronic barrier.

Upon the arrival of Jared, Garrett, and Thora – along with over one hundred Arianni defenders – Gunnar escaped his temporary cave prison and met immediately with the Arianni rescue squadron. His information as to how the Annunaki were deployed enabled Garrett, Jared and Thora to plan for an efficient, and possibly surprise surrounding of the elite guard of the Annunaki. With Gunnar directing the movement, the Arianni encircled the Annunaki soldiers and took up stealth positions of strength to protect against the invaders. Garrett issued an ultimatum to Muchin, informing him that his troupe was surrounded and urged them to surrender immediately.

Muchin, however, was never one to back away from a fight. Confident that his highly trained elite guard would never shy away from combat and could prevail, he gave the order to engage the Arianni with laser weapons. He refused to listen to any terms suggesting defeat and challenged the Arianni action by threatening to execute or torture some local humans as a demonstration of their resolve.

The warriors and their laser weapons were quickly neutralized by Arianni non-lethal technology, abruptly negating the overt threat. Several Annunaki warriors were stunned and the rest succumbed to the overwhelming weaponry superiority that they had experienced and quickly surrendered. In the skirmish, Muchin was taken captive.

As the Arianni consolidated their victory, it was apparent that they had accomplished what they were sent to do. The young leaders were gratified with their victory and were pleased that their mission was accomplished without bloodshed. They reasoned that their primary mission was a success. The captive Annunaki were imprisoned in the very cave where Gunnar and Roola had been held.

Thal received the news of the confrontation and told the rescue team that he would contact Goran and provide him with yet another ultimatum, to either cease his aggressive exploits on Earth, or be faced with an interplanetary war.

Goran reacted to Thal's demands with anger, resistance, and a desire for revenge. He threatened to execute Roola if Molea or the Arianni continued their overt actions. He accused the Arianni of deliberately and willfully ambushing his elite guard and capturing them, and demanded their immediate release. He questioned the motives of the Arianni and angrily challenged them to live up to their peaceful reputation.

Thal informed Lord Molea of the actions that were taken and, regretfully, informed him that his daughter, Roola, had been taken captive. Molea fell into an emotional quandary and asks Thal to support him in joint action procedures. A distressed Molea suggested to Thal that he be allowed to secretly return to Venus and contact loyal supporters to assist him in his quest to reassume power and to stop Goran from any further actions that would ignite an all-out war.

Thal cautioned Molea regarding the dangers inherent in his plan. He indicated that he would seek assistance from the Galactic Alliance that was formed for this very kind of event, but cautioned Molea of the inherent personal dangers involved with his mission. Thal informed Molea that the Arianni were already committed to removing any belligerent Annunaki from the disputed region.

****

Roola languished in the stark prison, not allowed any visitors or recreational exercise. Becoming somewhat depressed at her predicament, she tried to shut off her mind from focusing on the plight of both herself and her father. Her father was her hero, but she knew that if anything happened to him, she would step in to occupy the position of sovereign.

It was late in the evening when someone familiar appeared at the entrance of Roola's electronic cell. It was Plotus. He had heard from some of his faithful followers that she was being held by Goran.

"How are you doing, my dear? Are you feeling alright?"

Roola look up in complete surprise and uttered weakly, "What are you doing here? How did you get in?"

"That's not important now," replied Plotus. "All you need to know is that we are working to get you released as soon as possible. I wanted to check as to your physical and mental condition before we did anything that would be considered imprudent. A group of us are trying to find a way to bring your father back home to reassert his position and thwart Goran's maniacal actions. I was also imprisoned for even suggesting that we not provoke a war, but I still have support and friends in high places who have given me some leeway to operate for the common good.

"Be strong and be patient, dear Roola. All this will happen rapidly as we are attempting to contact Molea as we speak. I will get back to you as quickly as I can."

Chapter 8

AN EXTRAORDINARY PROJECT

*R*aggs was perplexed by the sudden disappearance of Thora and the complete of absence of communication from her. In his concerned curiosity, he decided to visit the home of Oliver and Jackie in an attempt to learn more about her whereabouts. He found it hard to believe that she would disappear without letting him know and he was worried about her. Their relationship had blossomed to a point where their mutual interest in one another had become more intimate and personal. Raggs felt a sinking in the pit of his stomach as he approached the house.

On arrival at the Hill household, he was struck by the fact that the house seemed unoccupied and there was no sign of anyone living there. The mail had gathered around the mailbox and some light cobwebs had formed in the corners of the front door indicating its lack of recent use. He considered calling the local police to help him find out what had happened to Thora, and perhaps Ollie and Jackie, but decided to postpone such action fearing he would be acting too hastily.

His frustration, however, led him to force entry into the home with the intention of searching for any clues as to their puzzling disappearance. He took the liberty of searching throughout the house, and especially Thora's room, hoping to uncover any information on where they all might have gone. He immediately noticed that the Holy Lance was missing from its normal place of honor on the wall above her dresser. This revelation triggered his concern even more. As he and Thora'a relationship had evolved, she had revealed the legend of the Holy Lance and her father and mother's mission to return it to the Hollow Earth residents. He left the house before drawing the attention of local authoritieis and made his way back to his classroom.

Back at his University classroom, where Raggs was finishing his semester teaching assignment, a very tall Nordic man suddenly appeared at the back of the room as his final class ended. The man approached Raggs slowly and deliberately, unsure of what Raggs' reaction would be. He was holding in his hand a folded piece of paper and had extended it towards the young teacher. As Raggs reached out to take the paper, Sven Olafsson stretched his massive frame to his full height and quietly introduced himself as a particular friend of Thora and her grandparents.

Raggs was awestruck by the spectacle of the enormous size of Sven and turned his full attentioin to the surprise visitor. Sven asked Raggs if he could speak to him in private. Raggs, shaken by the untimely arrival of this extremely impressive man, immediately recalled that he was the man Thora had referred to many times in previous conversations about her parents and the Hollow Earth. Raggs, without any objection, agreed to talk in private and led Sven into an adjoining office. They sat down and Sven began his story, presenting Thora's note to Raggs.

"My dear Raggs," the note began, "Please forgive me for not telling you where I am, but I had to depart suddenly. I am visiting the mountain, but want you to know that I am safe. You will be contacted by a tall, Nordic man who will explain my absence. My grandfather and grandmother are also here, safe, with me. Much love and blessings, Thora."

Raggs leaned back in his squeaky, oak office chair to contemplate what he had just heard from Sven and reflected thoroughly on the contents of the note. Thora was in Shasta! Impressed by the presence and the articulate manner of speech exhibited by his silver-toothed visitor, he instantly deduced that Sven was a legitimate liaison for Thora. Sven's friendly and astute demeanor put Raggs at ease. He reread Thora's note over and over.

"Thora has asked me to contact you," Sven murmured, "to ask you to seriously consider coming with me on an unusual adventure and joining her in Agartha. She wants you to assist her with an extraordinarily important project that could affect the peaceful status of the entire Galaxy."

Raggs sat back in his chair again to consider the impact of what Sven had presented to him. His thoughts were spinning, but the chance to be with Thora ignited his adventurous spirit. "This does not require much thought," he opined, as his job assignment had ended and there was nothing else occurring to compel him not to go. He looked directly at Sven and said, almost impulsively, "Yes, I will go with you. I am ready to leave when you are."

****

Raggs' arrival in Agartha confirmed that Thora's stories were not only true, but the city was much more fantastic even than she had related to him. Sven led him to the great reception hall where both Ollie and Jackie were there to meet him. Thora, they explained, was off on an Arianni mission with her father.

"Welcome to the center of the Earth," Jackie warmly greeted him, firmly grasping both of Raggs' outstretched hands. "Thora will be ecstatic that you are here. You have been very important in her life and she has missed you. We, for the time being, invite you to stay with us at our residence in The Colony. Thora will join us as soon as she returns from her assignment."

Relieved to know that his arrival was expected, as well as desired, Raggs relaxed, quickly at ease with Thora's grandparents. They had met a few times before as he and Thora were seriously dating one another and Jackie enthusiastically welcomed the reunion of the young couple. She admired and approved of the young man and his relationship with their beloved granddaughter.

A few days later, Thora arrived and was bursting with joy when she saw Raggs. "I was hoping you would come, but I wasn't sure you would be inclined to leave the familiar surface world and your work," she exclaimed, hugging him passionately.

"You are my incentive," Raggs gently responded. "I didn't need much more than that, and, of course, I was intrigued by Sven's invitation to assist in some mysterious galactic project."

"I will explain more on that later," cooed Thora, "but first let's sit down and I can bring you up to date on what has happened."

With that, Thora snuggled up to Raggs, delighting in the comfort she felt with him.

****

After a sumptuous meal prepared by Jackie, Thora sat down with Raggs to fill him in on the project that she and her father, Garrett, had initiated regarding developing a prototype of a fractal nitrogen generator.[1] As she was explaining the concept and his potential role in it, Raggs became more and more intrigued. His work in artificial intelligence and the exploration of unique planetary natural gases in his research made the project a natural fit for him. Thora explained that he would eventually be working with her Arianni cousin, Gunnar, as well as an ample number of middle Earth assistants, in a phenomenally well-equipped Arianni laboratory in Agartha. Thora emphasized the importance of the project and admitted she had enlisted Thal to help her convince Raggs to join the team. Raggs, however, needed no more convincing than Thora's request, and agreed to work with them for as long as necessary to achieve their goal. Raggs would start immediately and be joined by Gunnar as soon as Gunnar's release from the capture could be secured.

****

When Thal explained his nitrogen research proposal to Molea, the deposed leader asked if a team of loyal Annunaki scientists could be spirited out of Venus to participate. After brief consideration, Thal decided not to grant that privilege for Arianni security reasons. The generator, when developed, would be used as a bargaining chip to avoid a war, but the Arianni would not be comfortable with any alien assistance, let alone from the Annunaki. The implementation and development of fractal mathematics to power the nitrogen conversion system would become the focal point of the project.

The laboratory provided by the Arianni proved to be beyond state-of-the-art that either Raggs or Thora could have imagined. It was equipped with a myriad of electronic, magnetic, and vacuum apparatuses that could be used to test and manufacture just about anything that the young couple could imagine. The Arianni also provided more than adequate help from their own scientific community who contributed in building and assessing prototypes of technology, holographs, and experimental models.

The space was more than adequate, with living quarters attached to the Lab that allowed workers to rest and rehabilitate while working long hours in intense focus. Food was prepared in an adjoining room that provided all members rich and healthy meals during their sojourn. Raggs, Thora, and Gunnar, who had easily made an escape from the cadre of Annunaki who held he and Roola captive, were given full reign over the facility and were encouraged to utilize any avenue in pursuit of their goal.

Thora especially enjoyed that she was working with Gunnar, giving her time to get to know her alien cousin. And, of course, having Raggs working side by side with her fulfilled her dreams as she was certainly in love with her Icelandic partner.

Long hours working together in the lab tested not only the resolve in completing their task, but also tested and enhanced the developing relationship between Raggs and Thora. One evening after working well into the late hours, both decided they had had enough and would retire. Each had been given comfortable sleeping quarters and had spent several previous evenings resting and recuperating from the ordeal of experimentation and data analysis.

Just before retiring, Raggs placed a light tender kiss on the nape of Thora's neck. Thora reciprocated, smiling appreciatively and sharing a light squeeze of his hand. Hand in hand they walked to their adjoining rooms, each reluctant to break the physical bond.

Raggs stared lovingly into Thora's deep blue eyes and admitted quietly that he was in love with her. Still holding hands, Thora embraced him with her entire body, leaving no doubt of her mutual attraction.

"I love you too," she replied breathlessly. "I think I have loved you since that first day in the library. Being here with you only makes my feelings stronger. I want us to share our love, now, while we can. Who knows what the immediate future will bring with the pending conflict with the Annunaki?" She gently picked up Ragg's hand and placed it softly over her right breast. "Stay with me tonight," she whispered, "Let's be the lovers we are."

Raggs' feelings passionately intensified. This was a moment he had felt sure would come, but had wanted Thora to initiate that connection. After all, her mission was becoming her life and he did not want to interrupt or derail in any way her commitment to her parents and the Arianni.

"I want you to know that I wish to spend the rest of my life with you, no matter what our mission is. Wouldn't it be wonderful if we chose to be married, start a family, and enjoy all the marvels of being together?"

"Oh, I was hoping and praying you felt that way!" Thora sobbingly replied. "We are surely blessed at this moment."

With very little continued conversation, Raggs lovingly took Thora by the hand and together they retired for the night.

---

[1] Fractal Mathematics: Not until the computer became a useful tool did the concept of fractals take hold. In 1975, a French-American mathematician, Benoit Mandelbrot, was the first to observe the effect. Strikingly beautiful and infinitely complex images are generated by fractal formulae. The fractal images possess repeated self-similar patterns, regardless of the scale on which they are examined. The more magnified the images, the more the structure appears to be the same. Therefore, the Arianni lab workers were examining how fractal mathematics could replicate a nitrogen generating device that would repeat itself in growing its base, allowing for creating a series of devices that could handle large scale operations.

Chapter 9

CONFLICT IN SUBTERRANEAN VENUS

*G*oran paced the floor of his newly acquired leadership office and pondered the specter of an internal rebellion against him. He worried because he did not know who was with him and who might still be aligned with Molea. And, on reflection, he was puzzled by the less than enthusiastic support exhibited by Plotus and was becoming suspicious of what might be Plotus' inner thoughts and intentions. He concluded that Plotus was most likely a threat and, without further deliberation, seized Plotus and placed him under arrest for treason and other crimes. Other leaders, who had always respected the calm, guiding hand of Plotus under Molea, rallied behind Plotus after hearing of his arrest and began promoting subterfuge that began to permeate the Annunaki governmental and military societies.

Goran, however, paid little attention to these rumblings of dissent, and ramped up his plan to mobilize the Annunaki for war. He was determined to push on because of his deep belief that colonization on planet Earth was their only road to survival. The strength of his convictions would not be easily dismissed or delayed.

Roola was sequestered in the area prison designated for traitors, capital lawbreakers, and perpetrators of general crimes against the Annunaki culture. She was treated as an ordinary, common criminal at the behest and direction of the faux Lord Goran. Roola would be a useful hostage should any potential coup materialize. Goran ordered that she receive no special treatment and threatened to punish anyone who provided her any special status or comfort while in custody.

Roola did her best to adjust to the indignity of her incarceration, but was rapidly slipping into despondency, knowing that her life, and that of father, was in jeopardy. She intuitively contemplated the fate of her people who were largely unaware as to the impact of the recent coup against her father. She feared that events could quickly get out of hand, with the distinct possibility that a war could destroy both the Arianni and the Annunaki civilizations.

Goran had taken measures consolidate his power and leadership, assuring that a few of the senior military leaders were supporting him. Even with this minimal support, Goran was confident that his plan would succeed.

****

Molea was becoming more and more distressed at the evolving situation, fearing that his home planet would take a foolish action under Goran and attack the Earth and its inner kingdom. He was equally upset that his daughter was being held captive and her life was in grave danger.

The deposed leader arranged a meeting with Thal to ask his help to quietly slip back to Venus and attempt to thwart any plans for attack. He would enlist Plotus as an ally and try to convince the majority of military leaders, over whom he felt he still had some influence, that any attack was futile and could destroy the very civilization that they all were trying to save.

After listening thoughtfully to Molea's plan to return to Venus, Thal reluctantly expressed support even though it appeared to be an act of desperation and was unlikely to succeed. The list of other responses seemed equally futile – short of war.

Even though Plotus was imprisoned, he still had loyal followers who maintained regular contact with him. They also reestablished and kept the lines of communication open with Molea, hoping one day soon he would reassume his position as leader of the Annunaki. Through these loyal channels, Molea was able to organize assistance to orchestrate his pending return.

****

Molea's journey back to Venus was one filled with trepidation and fear. Molea knew he had to act quickly in order to to surprise Goran and his followers. The success of his mission required faultless thinking and maneuvering. Molea attempted to calm the explosion of powerful excitement within him when he contemplated the gravity of his undertaking. This would not be easy, but the call of destiny outweighed any concern of risk.

Molea's stealth arrival went smoothly. He was quickly spirited to a safe house where he could direct any overt or covert operation. How well could he trust the so-called loyalists to his cause? He had no choice, he thought; he had to act and let the cards fall where they will. He had recruited a cadre of soldiers to surprise Goran by slipping into the leadership confines by way of a secret escape tunnel that Molea had authorized some years back in anticipation of the need for a rapid escape route for him and his immediate lieutenants. He was confident that Goran was not aware of this clandestine escape route. The plan was for the armed cadre to quietly enter the cave, ascend the stone carved stairs and burst into the leadership room where they would seize Goran and reinstall Molea's sovereign leadership. Molea, waiting inside the cave's entrance, would follow as soon as the confines were secure. His cadre would eliminate any guards that remained loyal to Goran.

As the Molea contingent entered the cave and slowly made their way up the rough-hewn stone stairs to the leadership chamber, they felt confident that they would storm the chamber by surprise. Goran's elite guard, however, was aware of their entry. Unbeknownst to Molea, Goran had known for some time about the escape route and was setting a trap. One of Molea's so-called faithful soldiers had secretly reported to Goran and revealed the plot to him. Goran sealed off the upper secret door to the compound and directed another cadre of his men to secure the entrance to the cave. Molea and his troupe were trapped. As they began to fight their way back through the original entrance, they were thoroughly overwhelmed by laser weapons, killing most of the patriotic invaders and mortally wounding Molea.

The death of Molea portended a new era for the Annunaki. With Goran now firmly entrenched in his leadership role, the threat of an all-out war became a distinct possibility. Plotus and Roola were safely in custody and the future of their potential peaceful influence was in serious doubt.

Goran was delighted at the turn of events. His confidence grew, knowing that Molea was dead and Molea's successor, Roola, was safely in his custody. What could possibly stop him now?

Chapter 10

FRAGMENTED HUMANOIDS

*L*ong evenings working diligently to find the fractal formula to replicate nitrogen regeneration were proving to be a daunting task to the researchers. While the Arianni technological team seemed to thrive on the work, Raggs and Thora wearied with the long hours and sleepless nights running scenarios through their respective simulators hoping to find a key to unlocking the vast puzzle that spread itself before them. Raggs did his best to weather the recurrent routines of testing, recasting their formulas, and testing some more. Gunnar displayed his Arianni fortitude and ability to stay focused on the desired outcome and simply never complained.

Thora, however, was feeling the effect of the grueling requirements of the research and began to feel her body weakening. Headaches became more frequent and her attention span seemed to dwindle as the project wore on. Part of her weariness, she thought, was the fact that they were on the threshold of using fractal geometry, a discipline in which her expertise was limited. Driven by her need to complete the work, she persevered nevertheless while making small but significant errors in her calculations.

Raggs was first to notice the fatigue that Thora was exhibiting. When he asked her if she was all right, Thora passed off his concern by dismissing it outright. Subsequently, however, Raggs could detect a noticeable shift in her demeanor and took her aside to comfort her.

"My love," Raggs gently spoke, "You don't seem yourself. I think you are weary and don't want to admit it. Perhaps you need to take a break from this for awhile. The whole project, as you can see, is in very capable hands and we are nearing a significant breakthrough. Please take some time off to rest. We will all feel better if you do."

Thora's first reaction in her mind was to protest Raggs' assessment. Before she could speak, her mind and emotions let her admit that, indeed, she was exhausted and was not contributing much and was probably slowing down the group with her noticeably erratic energy flow. Thora reluctantly admitted to Raggs that she knew she needed a break. She decided to go to the Commons for a visit with Garrett and Gugga. On her way, she was delighted to run into Solaris who was relaxing at a cafe after a day of teaching.

Thora, after spending many intimate moments with Solaris, had become very comfortable in her new close relationship with the wise Arianni teacher. She marveled at the multiple talents that Solaris displayed with her vast knowledge of the language of stones. She peppered Solaris with a plethora of questions regarding how she began her role teaching those in the Arianni acculturation process.

The conversation drifted towards the origin of the Arianni. Thora began probing Solaris for what she knew about the early history of the subterranean dwellers.

****

Solaris sat back in her chair while sipping a hot beverage, spurred to reflection by Thora's interest. "Well, do you remember your first hours in Agartha when you were waiting in that large ornate room before meeting Thal? That building is the historical repository of documents and crystal writings regarding not only the origination of the Arianni, but also the ancient accounts of how the humanoid species began and evolved. The story is a fascinating one that explains why we Arianni insist that visitors and guests who wish to join us undertake what we call our acculturation process. That progression, hopefully, connects our current physical presence with the deeper spiritual integration of each of us.

"This habitation and all it contains is overseen and protected by one we call The Dweller, an androgynous being that lives deep in the Halls of Amenti, the center of our knowledge and storehouse of our accomplishments. The Dweller is available to provide us access to knowledge of the elders, access to the crystal-laden history of our world, and advice to our civilization. The history, of course, also includes you and all the surface dwellers as humanoid descendants. How much do you want to know? I have spent many, many hours pouring through the archives in order to understand where we came from, and more importantly, where we are headed as a species."

"I want to know it all!" Thora enthusiastically replied. "How did we humanoids begin? Where did we come from? Who else is in our Galaxy?"

"Hmmm," pondered Solaris before speaking. "Our more recent past, perhaps several millennia ago, if you can imagine a millennium as recent, began here on this planet. Our species established major civilizations in specific areas of the world. All of us came from the stars, specifically after further fragmentation,[1] namely from the star system of Sirius and the lure of Orion. We eventually settled here as well as on other planets. In our case, on Earth, there were two contrasting civilizations existing at about the same time. One was the technologically advanced and savvy group that settled on a continent the crystal archives call Atlantis. The Atlantians were obsessed with power and competition that led to their own demise through solar and atomic power culminating in a catastrophic war and the sinking of their continent into the Atlantic Ocean. The other continent, situated in the Pacific Ocean, was called Mu, or Lemuria.

The continent of Lemuria was also impacted in the cataclysmic far-reaching destruction of Atlantis, driving the inhabitants to seek refuge in the nearest habitable land masses. Most of the Lemurians migrated to the North American continent. Many took refuge in the center of the Earth through the portal located at what is now Mount Shasta.

"A number of Atlantians also escaped to the closest nearby continent of South America, also finding refuge in the caves and tunnels that catacombed from the eastern coasts to underground settlements on the west coast of South America. The Lemurians were a peaceful, thoughtful, and spiritual civilization and brought with them to the inner Earth the principles of peace and connection with nature.

"That was the genesis of our commitment to the acculturation process. Lemurians became known as Arianni and practiced the spiritual integration of the species. Learning from the lessons of Atlantis, we do not wish to fragment our society, but instead continue to build the forces of integration of all species without the negative connections of power, competition, and aggressiveness that often lead to war. We are, as a species, reluctant to engage in conflict as we know it diminishes us as well as those with whom we might fight. We will always seek the peaceful path of least resistance."

"Wow, that's fascinating," retorted Thora. "But where did we come from before Lemuria?"

Solaris set down her herbal tea on a nearby table, adjusted herself to fit the comfort of the chair, and said, "Now that is a truly remarkable story, Thora, one that stretches the limits of our minds, but shows us why we are here and who we are. It is the story of the evolution of the entire galactic humanoid species. Do you want to hear about the creation and what is known as the fragmentation of Lyra, the home of the original humanoids?"

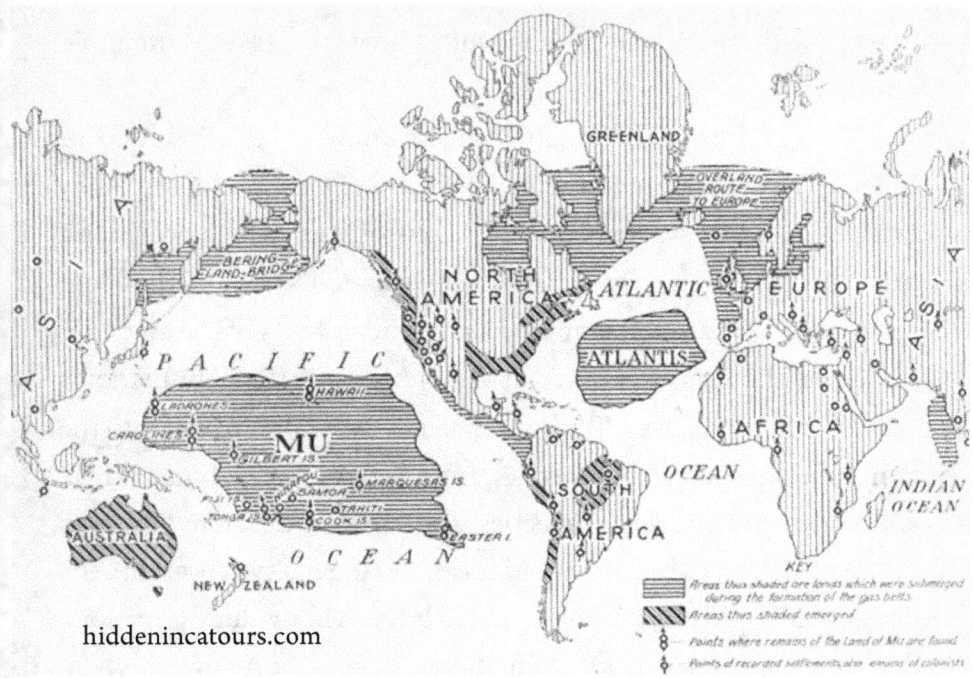

hiddenincatours.com

"Of course," replied Thora. "I have always been interested in ancient and spiritual history. Please start from the beginning."

"The evolution of the humanoid is rooted within the Galaxy,"[2] began Solaris. "There are many humanoid species that now reside in the Milky Way Galaxy, as the surface dwellers call it."

"Yes, but where did they come from?" Thora asked. "How were they created?"

"I'm getting to that," replied Solaris. "You should know that each humanoid species has the same general characteristics as the others, such as a torso, head, two arms and two leg appendages. Most humanoids, however, diverge from the core set of traits traits to reveal different shapes, sizes, skin types, color, and other unique features.[2] The Earth humanoid shares with all of them much of the same DNA, even as other strands may appear in their composition. For instance, one of the civilizations in the stars, the Vegans, experimented in gene splicing, but they only had one other species to work with, the reptiles. As a result, a new species of a humanoid reptile was created.

"The creators of all humanoids were known as the Founders or Elders. They represented the nearest ideal of God or Source. They existed in a white star (a white hole) constellation which provided a prism of light through which the first humanoids were birthed into existence. They are remembered as the inhabitants of the star constellation known as Lyra. Lyra is the mother star for all humanoids that exist in the Galaxy. The light through Lyra's prism split into the familiar color spectrum of Red, Orange, Yellow, Green, Blue, Indigo, and Violet, creating seven densities, also called dimensions, involved in the creation of the humanoid form. Each density represents the physical and spiritual station occupied by each individual humanoid, determining how it exists and functions. Most of the humanoids here on the planet Earth exist in the third dimension of density, while most of those in the Hollow Earth are concurrent travelers to and from the 5th and higher dimensions. All the dimensions have an integral relationship with one another, hence the quest to integrate back to the one actual being. All are striving for integration, the integration of the soul, a process of returning to our oneness, to our Source, to God.

"Legends suggest that the birthplace of humanoids began in the star cluster known as Lyra. However, the inhabitants of Lyra began to fragmentize and divide themselves into various polarized points of attraction. As a result, the fragmented beings of opposing polarities broke away from Lyra and migrated to a nearby star constellation known as Vega. Mind you, this was not just a physical fragmentation, but rather a psychological and spiritual split. Groups of Lyrans had differences and chose to leave Lyra and form a new civilization. As the fragmentations were rooted in spiritual and psychological thought, those that migrated to Vega also experienced the same phenomenon. Their fragmentation or split initiated another migration from Vega to a system called Apex. The story of Apex is one of tragedy because there the greed and power struggles led to the disappearance of the entire planet."

"What happened to them?" Puzzled Thora.

"They simply destroyed themselves, much like the seeds that preceded the destruction of Atlantis, followed by Lemuria," explained Solaris. "We Arianni view both historical cataclysmic events to be an archetypal lesson for our civilization here on Earth, a lesson on what greed, power and unbridled technology can produce. That is why we have acculturation. We believe humanoids can avoid those conflicts."

"Is that why you monitor the Earth surface dwellers, from a fear that their own competitiveness, greed, and power accumulation could affect the Arianni?"

"Precisely, that is the primary reason why we have invited you and your family to join us, so we can avoid such a catastrophe here. This will be your mission, or will be when the skirmish with the Annunaki is over. Dealing with the reptilians is not like dealing with other humanoids. Although we share some DNA, they vary greatly from us. We do know, however, that there are some prominent reptoids that share our longing for peace and tranquility and we will continue to explore those possibilities to preserve and enhance integration.

"Solaris," quietly whispered Thora, "What do the stones say about the Annunaki? Are they a major impediment to the success of integration?"

"The stones reveal a mixed future for planet Earth," answered Solaris. "I cannot decipher if the prediction relates to the interference of the Annunaki, or the Atlantean tendencies that are prominent on the surface. I do hear the stones echoing that a change is coming; what or where is unclear."

****

That night Thora retired to her room alone, falling into a deep sleep. She dreamed of a land of stones with keyholes of various shapes as she wandered searching for something with a sense of urgency. Upon awakening, she wondered what it could mean. Her intuition was strongly guiding her to take a break from the project for a time. She headed for the home of Gugga and Garrett.

Resting comfortably at the home of her parents, Thora redirected her mind to the vision she had received in her dream. She recalled her time in Iceland where, when she felt emotionally drained, she would meditate with her stone collection.

Gugga sat with her, holding her hand and comforting her daughter. After a moment, she squeezed Thora's hand and suggested, "Why don't you take a little vacation from the Commons? We can arrange to have you visit Iceland and perhaps reconnect with Meda, your childhood friend. I'm sure that Solaris might consent to accompany you. It would be a great time to reacquaint yourself with the stones. They've always soothed your soul when you consulted them."

"I'm amazed how you know what it is I am thinking," replied Thora. "In truth, I have been longing to see Meda so we can rekindle our friendship and revisit the connection we have with the stones. And I would love it if Solaris would accompany me. Her knowledge of stones is unsurpassed! Thank you for confirming my thoughts. I love you so."

---

[1] Fragmentation: Literally means "from the Source." It is the process of humanoids experiencing conflict amongst themselves, both physically and spiritually – and breaking away to establish a new paradigm in another star system. This process went on and on as each fragment would find a new constellation to live in and practice what they believed to be an impulse of their souls, leaving behind their civilization of origin.

[2] See Appendix III for a more complete discussion of the origin of humanoids. For more detailed information and knowledge of the evolution of the humanoid species, consult *The Prism of Lyra*, by Lyssa Royal and Keith Priest. Their channeling of the history of mankind is a detailed study of where we come from within the Galaxy and why we are here. Much of the information included here is gleaned from these studies. This work chronicles in detail the emergence of the reptiles in humanoid form, such as the Annunaki. (Light Technology Publishing, LLC, Flagstaff, Arizona, USA).

Chapter 11

ICELANDIC ADVENTURE

Solaris, soulmate of the magnificent Sven, was more than willing to accompany Thora to Iceland. She wanted to meet Meda and see where Thora spent her younger years. She had an additional request.

"Thora, I would like you, and perhaps Meda, to also come with me to Spitzbergen. It will be enlightening for you to experience firsthand where the great adventure of your dad and granddad took place."

"That would be wonderful! I would love to visit your and Sven's surface home. Maybe I can finally meet Loki. I think he and I will get along famously." Thora's imagination flared into a blaze of excitement at the thought of meeting the bear. The story of Loki's antics in rescuing the Lance from the marauders was a family favorite.

"I have no doubt that you and Loki will feel an immediate heart connection when you meet," said Solaris, "I haven't seen him for awhile and am looking forward to seeing how he is. He and Sven are so close. I sometimes wonder if Sven loves Loki more than me," she laughed.

"We'll make arrangements to go as soon as possible," Solaris thought. "We can show one another around and query the wisdom of the stones. I can't imagine a more exciting adventure."

The Arianni vacuum transport tube had routes that terminated at any point within the hollow Earth. The speed was so rapid that any entrance could be reached within minutes. Many eons ago, the tunnels were dug and fashioned by the early Lemurian elders when a pre-glacial civilization flourished on both sides of the Atlantic. Known as the Old Ones, they had the foresight to provide the many links and openings to the surface world.

****

Reykjavik, the capital city of Iceland, was as beautiful as ever. Surrounded by majestic mountains, caressed by the beautiful ocean, the city seemed veiled in an aura of peace and tranquility for all those who lived or visited there. Thora was proud to show her Arianni companion the sights of her native city and the heritage that she shared with her father and mother. For Solaris, the city reflected Thora herself, beautiful, quiet, peaceful and spiritually connected. She looked forward to visiting her home, which was still in the custody of Garrett and Gugga, and of course, meeting with her gemstone companion, Meda.

Thora was excited to have Solaris meet Meda. They arrived unexpectedly at the home of Meda's parents, Bjorn and Marit Ericsson. Although surprised, they were delighted to once again see Thora, embracing her while peppering her with questions about Garrett and Gugga. They had all become fast friends before Garrett went on his Holy Lance quest, and Bjorn was best man for Garrett at his wedding. Meda just happened to be visiting home while still completing her university education in Reykjavik. The delight in the two meeting one another again was palpable. After the introduction of Solaris, they all sat down to a hastily prepared meal of cooked rice and winter vegetables, all the while in rapt conversation both to catch up and talk about the future.

Thora couldn't wait to share with Meda the beautiful gemstone representative of her California Sierra Nevada mountains east of her grandparent's home in Berkeley. It was an Andara stone she had found while exploring her geological interests in the eastern Sierra range.

"What does it have to teach us?" Meda excitedly asked.

Thora knew that her friend understood the language of the stones.

"The Andara stone raises one's psychic sensitivity as it relates to extra-terrestrials," Thora explained. "And I have to show you the Amethyst crystal that Solaris had in her gem booth at our local county fair. The stone drew me to it immediately, letting me know that I was brought there for the purpose of connecting with Solaris and Sven. The stone directed me into an amazing story that has involved me in interplanetary connections. My life has been a whirlwind ever since."

Bjorn and Marit were fascinated. They were intimately aware of communication with stones due to the many experiences their daughter had shared with them over the years. Solaris produced the amethyst with its jutting violet crystals pointing upwards. She explained that she always consulted the amethyst to prepare herself for coming events. She mentioned that she and Thora were also going to Spitzbergen to gather other stones and to check on Loki, her companion Sven's pet polar bear.

"You are invited to join us, Meda. We're embarking on a special journey that we know you will enjoy. Of course, only if your parents are in agreement." As Solaris spoke the invitation, she experienced a flutter of knowing that, in fact, it was imperative that Meda accompany them. She was absolutely certain they were embarking on an adventure that would bring momentous consequences for the future, and that Meda's presence was required. While her heart raced with excitement, she maintained a calm air of nonchalance so as not to give Meda's parents any cause for concern.

"I think an adventure with the stones will benefit Meda right now, and we trust you to keep her safe," said Bjorn with Marit nodding in agreement. "How will you travel there?"

Thora and Solaris glanced at one another and grinned.

"We will utilize Arianni transport," Solaris explained. "The distance will be covered in just a few minutes. It is completely safe and the entrance is readily accessible in Reykjavik. We will, however, require you to keep this mode of transportation secret and we trust that you will do so. Garrett and Gugga assured me that you would not have a problem with that. Am I correct?"

"Of course," Marit said, "We are used to keeping secrets here. In fact it took some time and trust for us to alert Garrett and Gugga as to the existence of MIBs in Iceland. You can confide in us."

"When can we leave?" Meda asked. "I have just another week before I have to be back in school."

"We'll leave tomorrow," said Solaris. "I still want to spend a night at Thora's childhood home."

****

Entering the stealth Arianni transit tube was a fantastical experience for Meda. She was astonished that such a system existed, and with an entrance just below Reykjavik. This would certainly be a journey she would never forget. The very existence of her home town and her current life retreated to the back of her mind as she stepped into an entirely new world.

The journey of a few hundred miles to Spitzbergen took less than a few minutes. The three women exited the tube and stood for a moment gazing at the beauty of the small town. Sven's hanger and airstrip were just a brisk walk from the town center. Sven had fashioned a comfortable living space adjacent to the makeshift airport, although it had retained some of the odor of Loki who often slept inside. No matter though, the women were delighted to be sequestered in a warm comfortable environment.

The morning light produced a welcome to a new day. As the women awoke, they happily feasted on some provisions that Sven maintained in the abode. Thora and Solaris shared with Meda the challenge of the nitrogen generator project that was underway to avert a conflict with the Venusians.

Meda's face lit up as the reality of the situation struck her. "I understand now why you came to find me. Whatever is happening right now feels momentous...Are you feeling it too?"

Tuning in to the gravity of the situation, the three women simultaneously realized that their coming together at this time was for more than a pleasant diversion, but rather was the undertaking of a mission. As they sat in meditation that morning, a shared vision arose directing them to go out to the mountains near the ice floes where each one would collect a stone that promised a special revelation.

****

Loki peered curiously at the home and wandered over to investigate. When he saw Solaris, a frequent visitor and beloved consort of Sven, he let out a delightful roaring cry that startled both Meda and Thora.

"Oh, that's Loki," calmed Solaris. "Oh my goodness!" she cried. "He has a mate with him and I see two cubs trailing his mate. What a surprise! I can't wait to tell Sven. He will be thrilled."

Loki approached the house and nudged the front door with his ample snout. He snorted as the door swung open, leaving the two young women frozen in place as they marveled at the size and apparent friendliness he exhibited towards Solaris. A short distance behind the massive beast, his mate followed Loki's lead and was gentle and inquisitive – unusual behavior for a mother bear with cubs in tow.

Staying close to Loki's mate, the two young cubs were raucously playing with one another, each wrestling the other to the ground and unconcerned about their human companions. Their curiosity upon noticing the strangers, however, got the best of them and they bolted towards the women with playful exuberance.

It was a bit disconcerting to have four bears at their door entrance, yet there was no feeling of fear or threat to any of the women. Loki was very attentive to Solaris, licking her on the face while Solaris laughed and giggled at the antics of her furry friend.

"Let's call her Yoki," gushed Thora. "They'll be a couple – Loki and Yoki. Let's name the cubs Jack and Jill in tribute to their propensity of continually tripping over each other," she laughed.

The bears settled down quickly, satisfied that the humans were friendly and loving. Taking the lead of Loki, they nestled themselves in the snow in front of the house as if they were on guard. The two younger women stayed on the porch marveling at the presence of the pure white animals. Solaris went back inside to bring a treat for their new companions. All four of the bear family shared some dried fish that Solaris split among them.

"Let's eat something before we go on our stone expedition," Solaris suggested. "We don't want to be caught in the wilderness without sustenance," she opined as she packed some additional dried food in her tunic. As they were preparing to leave, all three simultaneously felt the sensation of a wave of energy flowing through their bodies as sunbeams streaked across the morning-lit room. They were moved to spontaneously join their index fingers to form a unique bond and create a pact to have courage and keep one another safe.

The day was chilly, the sun barely visible behind some thick Arctic clouds. There was a slight wind that blew into their faces while they walked, but not so serious that it thwarted their plans. They were dressed warmly without the bulk of heavy skins for warmth, as Solaris had brought with her some loose-fitting garments fashioned by Arianni technology that promised to keep them warm on their trek. Each of the women donned their temperate suits just before leaving, toting a small backpack filled with drinks and food.

They weren't going to travel far, but far enough that they had to be cautious of the ever-shifting weather patterns of the area. The wind chill alone could make their trip miserable if they had to stay in it for a sustained amount of time.

The moment they left the house, the bears, almost on cue, pulled away from their comfortable snow beds, and began to follow. Meda and Thora were delighted that the bears were so protective and would want to accompany them.

The chilling wind became stronger and more biting as they continued, but none of them felt the need to return to the house as the lure of the stones was paramount on their minds. With her longtime expertise in psychic work, Solaris guided the group to stand in a circle, raise their vibration to the highest frequency possible, and offer an intention to discover a stone with useful properties. The three fanned out, and soon each had been guided to select a particular stone. Meda, however, was beginning to feel the effects of the cold on her slim body. She began shivering and her outer facial skin was displaying a bluish tinge, even under the cover of her warming garment. Solaris noticed the change in Meda right away and insisted they turn back home. Thora agreed as Meda nodded her head also.

Meda was getting colder every minute. By the time they arrived at Sven's abode, she was shaking violently from the cold. Her feet and hands were numb and she could barely talk, and certainly wasn't thinking clearly. It was obvious that Meda's warmth suit was failing.

Once inside and out of the wind and cold, Thora and Solaris

began heating water and wrapped Meda in a series of blankets while they disrobed and engulfed their bodies around Meda. In the midst of their ministrations, Meda suddenly became lucid and began to speak as if in trance. "The stones want us to know that they hold the answer to the project your team is working on in the inner Earth."

Stunned, Thora wanted to ask questions but Solaris squeezed her hand urging her to be silent, as Meda spoke another cryptic message. "Thora, your stone is Kano, first... Solaris', your stone, Ehwaz, second, and my stone is Dagaz, three." At that, Meda lost consciousness.

While Thora and Solaris continued to warm the body of Meda, a remarkable incident occurred. Loki, who had been observing curiously the actions of the women, pushed open the front door and sauntered his way over to Meda and wrapped himself around Meda somehow instinctively to give her warmth. Solaris and Thora were dumbfounded and backed away from the bear's action. As Solaris quickly jotted down what she could remember of Meda's strange transmission, Loki positioned himself to hold Meda to his warm stomach area. He stayed with her until Meda's body temperature rose to a safe level before he unceremoniously got up and ambled back outside. Meda awakened from her sleep while still in the embrace of the huge ice bear, watching in amazement as Loki gently released her and withdrew. Loki had saved her. Meda struggled to stay awake, but fell quickly back asleep.

After a protracted sleep, Meda woke up to find Thora and Solaris quite relieved to know she had recovered. The two of them hovered over Meda, and when the time was right, told Meda about the trance she had experienced and what she had spoken about the stones holding an answer to the nitrogen development project that was currently at an impasse.

"Wow!" Meda exclaimed. "I've always known I had an attraction to the stones, and I feel there is a message somewhere in this for me too. Thank you for taking such good care of me." She gazed at Solaris and Meda with deep gratitude.

They each placed their stone on the table in front of them, while they feasted on potato and rice soup with some warmed winter vegetables that Sven had put away for just such an emergency. After their ordeal, each remarked that the food, as plain as it was, was the finest meal they could have imagined.

Then the three women put their attention on the stones they had collected, excited to delve into the mystery of what had happened on the mountain. Thora quickly recognized that Meda had spoken the names of ancient Runes: Kano, Ehwaz and Dagaz.

"One, two, and three..." said Thora. A shudder went through her body as she recalled the story her father had told of the Runic triangle that opened the passage to the Hollow Earth while he was being pursued by hostile planes over the Arctic Circle.

"That's it!" Thora exclaimed with excitement. "We need to get these stones back to the inner Earth right away. They have something to do with the solution to the project."

Solaris sent quick telepathy to Sven, alerting him to let the team know that the women had received information that would assist in bringing the solution to the nitrogen generation puzzle.

They then tuned in to the stones more deeply.

Solaris and Thora, both experts in identifying stones, immediately recognized and identified each. Thora's stone was Amethyst. The stone Solaris had been given was Garnet, while Meda's stone was Obsidian.

"This is quite a lovely group of stones," observed Solaris.

"Tell us about them Solaris," beamed Meda, now fully warm. "What are they and what do they mean? How do they speak to us?

What do they say?"

Solaris methodically picked up each, one at a time, and cupped her hands around caressing the energy of the stone.

"You will recognize this one, Thora. It was like the one I was handling when we first met. Do you remember?"

"Oh yes," Thora responded. "I will never forget the message it sent me. It told me that I met you for a reason, but I didn't know what at the time, or not until Sven revealed himself. This particular amethyst geode is smaller and needs to be opened to reveal the violet/purple crystals inside."

"What does it mean?" asked Meda.

Solaris answered first. "The amethyst is a balancer. It balances the physical, mental and emotional bodies, linking them to the spiritual, cleansing the Aura. That was the effect it had on Thora when we first encounter the gem together. It is beautiful, is it not?"

"And this one is Garnet," interjected Thora, as she held the stone Solaris had brought back, repeating the procedure of cupping the stone within her hands and closing her eyes. "Garnet is known for bringing courage and hope into seemingly hopeless situations. It encourages letting go of old ideas and brings confidence."

"And this one…" Solaris continued, holding the stone Meda had chosen, "…is Obsidian – a stone without boundaries or limitations. It serves to expose flaws, weaknesses and blockages. Somehow, these stones in combination hold the key to our puzzle!" She sighed with amazement as the three stones were placed in a triangular formation. All three women immediately noticed a frequency engulfing the room as they sat gazing at the stones.

"We need to get these stones to the inner Earth team as quickly as possible!" the three said almost simultaneously.

"I'm glad you are fully recovered, Meda," said Solaris. "I hope your parents will forgive us for exposing you to the harsh elements of Spitzbergen. But it's clear that your experience on the mountain, even though it was life-threatening, was an important sort of initiation for you."

"Yes, I can see that forces were at work to open me up to a deeper understanding of stones and my own abilities to receive information from the unseen realms. We don't have to make it as dramatic as it was, but of course I can't wait to tell them about Loki and Yoki and the two cubs, Jack and Jill."

They all laughed recalling the antics of the four bears, yet keeping in mind the protective human-like reaction of Loki in warming Meda and keeping her from hypothermia.

"It's time now for Solaris and me to head back to the Commons," said Thora as she gazed into Meda's eyes. "It's been a momentous two days, and I'll never forget this experience we shared."

They gathered their belongings and said their hugging goodbyes to Loki and his family. After a brief stop in Reykjavik to bid farewell to Meda nd her family, Solaris and Thora were transported back to the Commons.

Chapter 12

THE BETRAYAL

*T*he Annunaki and the Royal Teutonic Knights were never political allies. They, however, were aware of one another's existence
through their respective dealings with Thal and the Arianni, yet had
never broached any attempt to coordinate or communicate between
them. Both groups were aware of the plight of the other – each des-
perately attempting to address and solve their respective crises. They
had not considered the potential advantage of an unholy alliance that
might be struck to fulfill the needs of both. Desperate circumstances
would soon conspire to effect a change in their relationship.

Goran, who was more willing due to the time pressure on his
need to take action, took the first step. He reasoned that he could
send an emissary to Wewelsburg Castle to suggest a quid-pro-quo
alliance that would help them get information from the Knights on
how to successfully enter the Hollow Earth and wreak havoc on the
middle realm. In turn, Goran would assist the Knights in obtaining
the Holy Lance, which he knew was either in the possession of Thora
or the Arianni and would be easily seized once they gained entry
into the middle Earth. After all, the Annunaki were not interested
in an earthly power symbol. They considered such artifacts as folly.

Goran dispatched his most loyal lieutenant, Chiron, a skilled
Annunaki negotiator, to shape-shift into human form to make a
proposal.

As Chiron arrived at the gates of Wewelsburg Castle, he was

greeted by castle guards who sequestered him in an adjacent room with comfortable sitting arrangements where he was served a warm beverage to offset the chill of the cooling nights and the chilly castle.

Arrangements had been made for him to meet with Ritter Von Zant, the titular leader of the Teutonic society. While puzzled by the nature of the possible agenda of the Annunaki negotiator, Von Zant had been alerted by Goran that Chiron was coming, appearing in human form so as to not disturb those associated with the castle.

"Greetings," Chiron spoke while extending his hand in friendship. "I am here as the representative of the Annunaki to talk to you and perhaps strike a bargain that will be of mutual benefit to both our agendas."

"Welcome to Wewelsburg," Von Zant replied. "I have been curious as to the reason for your visit and look forward to what your new leader, Lord Goran, may have in mind. I admit I cannot imagine a mutual interest that would prompt this meeting, but I'm always willing to explore possible new alliances."

"I'll get right to the point," Chiron replied. "We do indeed have a mutual interest! Some years ago we met up with one of your Knights, a Reichsmarine Captain named Otto Wermoutt. We believe he can be of service to us and we believe we can assist you in the return of the Holy Lance, which I know you covet. Is he still a part of your organization?"

Von Zant pondered what to say next and then stated unequivocally, "Yes, Ritter Wermhoutt is still a trusted member of our organization."

"I am aware that he is a resident of the Commons, near Agartha," continued Chiron, "And if he can provide us with important information, we will be in a position to assist you in retrieving the Holy Lance. We, of course, have no interest in the Holy Lance itself, but if we are able to enter the Arianni sanctuary, we will be in a position to seize the Lance and return it to you."

The Ritter, somewhat surprised by the proposal, replied thoughtfully back to Chiron, "That is an interesting proposition. How do you know you can do it?"

"We are aware that a young couple escaped to the Middle Earth with the Lance and that you unsuccessfully gave chase. We know that the couple's daughter is now in possession of the Lance and we know where it is kept. We can get it for you if we are able to pierce the entrance of the Middle Realm. What we need from you is for the Captain, who we know is living in the Commons near Agartha, to find information on how to do so. As you can see, this could be of immense mutual benefit for all of us. My leader, Lord Goran, is anxious to hear your reply and agreement to this proposal."

"Hmm," thought Van Zant to himself, "This could be the opportunity that we have been waiting for."

"I will consult with my Board of Leaders and give you an answer later this evening. In the meantime, we will make you comfortable with rest, food and drink, while the Board confers."

Von Zant excused himself from his guest and immediately called together the resident Ritters, who constituted the Teutonic leadership Council, and presented Goran's proposal.

"Does he know the clandestine status of Ritter Otto, and the fact that he is working for us under a ruse that he was excommunicated from the Order?" asked Ritter Friedrich.

"I don't know if he does or not, but I suggest that we not mention the relationship between us and Ritter Otto. They do not need to know that. I will contact Ritter Otto as we agreed to do once new information regarding the Lance came to light. This may be an opportunity that will assure our success in meeting our objective.

Ritter Otto has been waiting patiently in the Commons, undergoing Arianni acculturation, which I know he is rejecting, waiting for a chance to act. I will inform Chiron that we will accept this proposal and ask him to relay to Goran that we will begin immediately.

****

Otto Wermhoutt received the news from the Teutonic Knights by private electronic communication. A sardonic smile crossed his face as he contemplated the gravity of this proposal. It had been a few years since the pursuing Teutonic Knights had been rescued from the ice floes by the Norwegian Navy. He remembered how Ritter Von Zant had commissioned him to remain in Spitzbergen until rescued by the Arianni patrol. His loyalty was resolute. The pursuit of the Holy Lance had dominated virtually every thought that crossed his mind since that dreadful day in Spitzbergen. The embarrassment of being outwitted and humiliated by a polar bear was deeply implanted within his mind. He had recurring dreams of that day, the Lance almost in his grasp, when Loki snatched it from him and ran out over the ice floes with the Lance clenched firmly in his jaws. Wermhoutt hadn't known at the time that the Lance that Loki grabbed was a replica and the actual Lance was on its way to the Hollow Earth.

The Captain welcomed the challenge that was presented to him by his long-time friends and colleagues – the Ritters of the Teutonic Order. He vowed to give the mission his rapt, loyal, and immediate attention. At last, he thought – a time for redemption. He was glad that he had met with Oliver Hill and broken the ice with him. Through him, Wermhoutt thought, he could find a way to communicate with his daughter and granddaughter to discover how to shut down the entrance defenses. They were working closely with the Arianni to develop a nitrogen generator. Surely, they would know the Arianni signal to gain entry into the Inner Earth sanctum.

Chapter 13

TECHNOLOGICAL TRIUMPH

Ollie and Jackie were the first to welcome Thora and Solaris back at the Commons. They were relieved and delighted to see Thora appearing fully rested and glowing with a radiance of excitement unlike anything they had seen in her for some time. Thora's mother and father, Garrett and Gugga, soon arrived, anxious for news about their home visit and the sojourn in Spitzbergen. Sven appeared on the scene, warmly embracing Solaris. Both Thora and Solaris gleefully related the whole incident with Loki and the incredible antics and rescue he performed with Meda. Thora marveled about Loki's new mate who they had named Yoki, and the two romping cubs named Jack and Jill. Because the three women had agreed to the names, they said laughingly, Sven would have to agree also. Sven grinned at the news and was obviously delighted that Loki was well and had received the three women warmly. This special bear, once again, had shown his uncanny ability to somehow understand a tense situation and taken it upon himself to revive Meda in his own unique way.

But once the pleasantries of their adventure and the joy of their return were shared, Solaris, with a knowing glance at Thora, quickly excused herself and urged Sven to return with her to their dwelling. Thora immediately queried her family on the status of the project.

"I must know…" Thora said with a note of excitement in her voice, "Has there been a breakthrough in the project in my absence? Tell me about the progress of the team."

"Unfortunately, the team has been faced with obstacle after obstacle and the project has basically come to a halt," Garrett shared. "The mood of the team is quite bleak."

Thora felt a surge of heat spring from the little drawstring bag attached to her belt. The three women, Solaris, Thora, and Meda, who had been the recipient of a transmission regarding the stones they had collected and their meanings, had made careful notes as they wrapped each of their stones in moleskin and placed them into one of the stone-collecting bags plentiful in Sven's abode. Thora had become the obvious caretaker of the bag and it's contents, and she had not let it out of her sight since their time together in Spitzbergen.

"I know this may sound strange to you," said Thora with an aura of mystery in her voice, "But we three women went on a trek into the mountains near Sven's home, where were each guided to select a particular stone. Then inexplicably, Meda became suddenly and severely affected by the cold and while she was experiencing hypothermia entered a trance state and gave us information about the stones. It was quite incredible!"

"But what does this have to do with the project?" Garrett and Gugga asked with excitement and interest.

"The message Meda received identified the three stones as *first*, *second*, and *third* along with a Nordic name for each stone: Kano, Ehwaz, and Dagaz. We figured out that the names are the names of Runes. Is it possible that the stones may be a Runic triangle that has something to do with the nitrogen generation project?" Thora related breathlessly.

Garrett and Gugga, as well as Ollie and Jackie, knew the latent power of a runic triangle that had opened the way for their descent into the Hollow Earth.

"We must get this information to the team right away!" said Garrett, turning to his daughter with a look of pride. "It clear that's why you left the project and went to Iceland with Solaris…You were on a mission of your own while we spun our wheels here, but that doesn't surprise me!"

"We will come with you," said Gugga, emphatically gesturing toward Garrett, who nodded in agreement. "You know we have experience with Runes. We'll meet you in the lab as soon as we can get there. There's something I need to do first."

"Please get a message to Solaris and ask her to meet us there!" Thora said to Jackie.

Jackie embraced her granddaughter, looking into Thora's eyes as she said, "I know you must be excited to see Raggs again. He has been worried about you. He is a wonderful and thoughtful young man, and we're so happy you have found someone who cares for you as much as he does."

"I've missed him so much," Thora responded as the others hugged her and said their goodbyes.

Thora made her way to the lab without delay. All who worked there greeted her enthusiastically and were delighted to see her back to normal and flashing her big smile to all present. She ran immediately to Raggs, who was seated at a table wearing earplugs while piecing together some generator parts. His startled response was one of delight as he held her close and kissed her, in front of his working colleagues who smiled with approval. Gunnar, usually quite reserved, grinned widely as he caressed his alien cousin warmly.

Brushing aside the pleasantries and her joy of the reunion with Raggs, Thora's demeanor became serious as she asked about the progress of the project.

"We've hit a roadlbock in our development of a prototype of a generator that can sustain itself," Raggs said, chagrined that he did not have better news. "We managed to adapt a model repetitive fractal formula that has enabled us to get to a certain point with the prototype. You were a part of that development process. The obstacle that existed when you left a few days ago is still plaguing us. We are scheduled to test it anyway tomorrow and we've invited Thal to come and witness our test. We've done our best to keep our hopes up, but we fear the test may be a disappointment."

At that moment, Gugga and Garrett arrived, followed not long thereafter by Solaris and Sven, who had made their way as quickly as possible when they received Thora's request. Solaris was expecting to be summoned, and had brought with her the formulary of encoded messages relating to the ancient Runes, as well as her handbook on the properties of gemstones.

At the arrival of the visitors, work had ceased as the entire lab team gathered around the group, sensing something monumental was about to take place. After briefly orienting the lab team as to what had taken place during her travel to Iceland, Thora gave instructions to set up a clear area near the device where they could work with the stones, and to inititate the steps to power up the apparatus to the point of activation.

Gugga quickly spread a woven cloth she had brought from her home. Thora opened the bag and unwrapped the stones, and respectfully, but without undue ceremony, laid them out in a row in the order "first, second, third" as Meda had received. Solaris spoke aloud, invoking the properties of the three Runes in conjugation with the harmonic aspects of the gemstone. As she did so, a blue-green flame of light appeared above the line of stones.

The three women stared in awe at the scene, awaiting a sign from the science team that the generator was triggering . Alas, there was no response.

Suddenly Garrett exclaimed, "Of course! It's a Runic Triangle similar to the one we were given that allowed us to enter the Hollow Earth some years back."

Thora immediately arranged the stones with the first at the top, and the second and third stones as the positions of a triangle. Solaris repeated the invocation, and at this point, a red/orange flame of light appeared next to the first flame, while a strange frequency began to flow across the room. There was still no activity from the generator. What was missing?

Momentarily stymied, the visitors gazed at the incredible scene, unwillingly to believe that Meda's vision was not going to yield the solution to the puzzle.

"Perhaps it needs an activator stone... like the one... like *this* one that I brought from our rooms following a streak of intuition."

Gugga extracted the activator stone from her bag and handed it to Thora. She raised it high and placed it in the center of the triangle.

At that moment, a complete light spectrum wave flowed like a curtain through the room, engulfing the occupants and creating a frequency channel that triggered the generator to begin humming.

In a short while, the apparatus was in full conversion mode nitrogen production, opening the way for the next steps of storage and transport to be undertaken.

A cheer went up in the room, as the visitors realized the import of their contribution, and the science team let go of the tension that had been mounting from their repeated failures.

Indeed, it was a day for celebration.

****

The next day, Thal enthusiastically witnessed a succesful test of the generator. "I'm so proud of all of you," Thal pronounced. "It's no surprise that the missing component is something out of the Arianni 5th dimensional reality field. It truly takes all of us together, working 'outside the box' to solve these kinds of challenges.

"I will inform the Galactic Alliance that a means for rebuilding the inner atmosphere of Venus has been found. This victory will open doors for other inner planets that have atmospheric issues, perhaps even our own one day.

"I plan to immediately contact Lord Goran to inform him of this feat an arrange for him to come here for a demonstration."

Over the next two days, the design team worked around the clock and succeeded in creating the final component to the nitrogen generator: a frequency duplicator that replicated the effect the Runes had demonstrated. The system could now be transported to Venus for permanent installation, when the time was right.

Chapter 14

THE UNRAVELING

It wasn't long before a detailed report on the project was conveyed to Goran. As he digested the report, he knew that if the generator actually worked it would not only preserve his civilization, but open new opportunities for him to solidify his newly acquired sovereign position. His thoughts opened to new dreams of Galaxy conquest under his leadership.

As Goran poured through the possibilities of his planet's salvation, he focused on the personal opportunity that this new discovery presented. While he assumed he was firmly in control of the Annunaki leadership, he worried about how the Alliance would view the abduction of Roola, who by virtue of sovereign rights was the rightful new leader of the Annunaki following the death of her father, Molea.

"I cannot afford to go to Agartha with the risk that I would be detained, stripped of my leadership, and forced to abdicate to Roola," he confided to his newest Lieutenant, Moro. Moro, he believed, was the only Molea holdover general who was trustworthy. He had shown his loyalty in the manner in which he handled the incarceration of Roola. It was obvious to Goran that Moro had a dislike for Roola and seemed to support both his leadership and the relocation of the Annunaki on Earth, even if it meant a major conflict with the Arianni.

"You cannot go to Agartha and risk your own arrest," pleaded Moro. "We need to request that the demonstration be held in a neutral area, perhaps the far side of the Earth's moon. There are many intact structures there that were left behind by early Sirius settlers that can be used for such a purpose, and we can assure our own safety. We, at this juncture, do not know whether or not we are being led into a trap."

"You are right, Moro. We need to be careful, but we cannot afford to miss an opportunity not only to protect our planet, but to gain the ability to penetrate the defenses of the Arianni. Perhaps I can insist that Captain Wermhoutt also attend the demonstration giving me a chance to hear what he has learned about the vortex that protects the Inner Earth entrances. He is still a member of the Teutonic Order and we have a deal. If we have that information, we could be unstoppable. Do you agree?"

"Absolutely," approved the newest Goran ally. "This mission of demonstration might open the pathway to our destiny, the leadership of the entire Galaxy."

****

When Thal heard the conditions that Goran put on the demonstration process, he immediately suspected that there was more to Goran's agenda than was apparent on the surface.

"Why," he pondered, "Would he insist the Captain be there? What possible connection could he have with the Annunaki? This demonstration will save his civilization. It would obviate any need to settle on Earth. How could he turn it down?"

Thal reasoned, however, that the invention was too important to the Galaxy to spend valuable time worrying about what Goran was thinking. There was nothing Goran could do, Thal rationalized, that would threaten the Arianni, as he certainly would agree to accept the results of the demonstration to save his planet. Thal agreed with the conditions, meeting on the far side of the Earth's moon to conduct the demonstration. He would have Thora and Garrett meet with the Captain to ascertain what Goran's strange insistence of the presence of the Captain might mean.

Still rejoicing with the success of the generator project, Thora and Raggs were puzzled as to why Thal requested that they, Gugga, and Garrett, meet with the Captain. Thal's reasons were somewhat vague as he asked them to interview the Captain and find out what relationship he had with the Annunaki.

"I don't know what Thal is looking for," interrupted Gugga. "But Wermhoutt has never been trustworthy as far as I'm concerned."

Garrett was pondering the question and reflected back on his time at Wewelsburg Castle. He remembered the Captain morphing his Teutonic Knight's image into that of Adolf Hitler during his initiation ceremony, a moment that had never left his mind over the years. Gugga's feelings were not to be discounted. She had many clairvoyant moments that taught Garrett not to ignore what she felt. And he, too, harbored many of the same emotions of distrust. Perhaps one or both of them would be able to see the real Captain, whoever he seemed to be.

Captain Wermoutt, home in his bungalow in the Commons of Agartha, stretched back in his comfortable easy chair, a chair especially constructed for him by Arianni craftsmen. He felt that his influence was that of a trusted advisor who stood in good stead with Thal and other Arianni leaders. He, therefore, was not surprised when Garrett contacted him with the offer to meet with his daughter and granddaughter. It was just a matter of time, he pondered. They would eventually come to him. Thora would be too curious to meet her maternal grandfather to wait any longer to initiate a meeting. This would provide an outstanding opportunity for him to find a way to have them give him information on the secrets to entering and exiting the Inner Earth openings. He would have the opportunity to serve the Teutonic Knights once again rather than continuing his ruse of acculturation.

The next day, the group met in a town hall community center so they could exchange greetings and stories. All of the participants, however, had their own secret agendas. The family wanted to unveil whatever the Captain seemed to be hiding, and the Captain wanted information on how the entry into the inner kingdom could be achieved.

Each of the group was on their best behavior, acting as though they were old friends who were meeting as a large family to reconcile any issues that may linger.

Garrett began the conversation.

"Well, we have been through a lot together. How are you adjusting to the Commons, Otto?"

"I have found it to be a great delight. Thal has treated me with the highest respect and has given me permission to enter and exit whenever I choose. I could not have it any better . . . and my acculturation progress has been significant. How have you all adjusted?"

Each related accommodating stories of their time in the Commons, often repeating the same pleasantries as the others. The conversations were cordial and informative. The Captain related some of the experiences he encountered in entering and exiting the inner Earth to visit areas on the surface.

"I have had the opportunity to travel to the surface and not be detained by anyone. It seems as if I hold some secret power, of which I have no knowledge or awareness of, to come and go as I please. I still haven't found the secret that allows me to do so."

Gugga listened carefully to the words of the Captain. "You realize, of course, that there is no secret, do you not?"

"What do you mean?" asked the Captain, becoming suddenly aware that he was about to learn the answer to his basic question.

"You must remember in the acculturation process, the teachers told us that the elders and founders, when they first came here, installed a spiritual filter that permeates all the entrances to the Hollow Earth. Every sentient being that comes through the entrances or exits is subject to this filter. It requires no guarding or maintenance as it is not penetrable except by the elders. When a being goes through the vortex, the filter picks up the resonance of the being and either lets him through or rejects him according to his present vibration. Any material object is also thwarted by the same process. To completely understand the process, one must reach a certain level of higher acculturation, something that none of us, apparently, have achieved. Were you not taught this during the early lessons of your acculturation classes?"

"No, I wasn't aware of that," sheepishly remarked the Captain while repositioning himself nervously in his chair.

"That's strange," said Gugga. "All students were made aware of that early on and are continually reminded. The teachers say that this is among the first understandings of living in the Arianni culture."

The Captain sat quietly absorbing the information. No, he was not aware the content of the lessons because he seldom attended classes and when he did, he paid little attention as his focus was with the goals of the Teutonic Knights, not acculturation.

The group was aware that they had spent most of the afternoon together and began to grow restless to conclude the rendezvous. Thora, after meeting her Grandfather, was becoming ill at ease. She and Gugga exchanged knowing glances as they all got up to leave. The trust was still not there and, if there was any potential for trust, it had quickly evaporated.

"Did you see him squirm when you told him about the entry and exit procedures? Why wouldn't he have known that?" remarked Garrett, "Did you notice how casually he brought the subject up? It was if he was trying to elicit information from us. I'm surprised he didn't bring up the nitrogen generator, as it is the latest major achievement and the worst kept secret on the planet. Once again, I believe he is hiding something."

****

Goran's plan began to take shape. With the consensus that the meeting and demonstration would be held at a neutral site, the far side of the moon, he detailed his scheme to Moro.

"I will go to the demonstration site and act grateful and thankful that the Arianni have found a way to save and sustain the civilization of the Annunaki. I will then accept the Arianni generosity and arrange to bring the device home to Venus."

His plan, however, was to set in place a demonstration of his oxygen depletion weapon that they developed some years back while experimenting with nitrogen generation. This weapon would immediately deprive the enemy of the life giving substance. As soon as he landed back on Venus, he would dispatch a stealth spacecraft that would activate the depletion device and force the Arianni to take him seriously. By this time, he would have already assured himself of taking possession of the newly created nitrogen generator and be prepared to activate it, while concurrently proceeding with his plan to pursue the demonstration. Timing was all important. He had to act before the Arianni could react to the oxygen depletion. It was apparent that his deal with the Teutonic Knights and Captain Wermhoutt did not bear any fruit due to the Captain's relaying that the entrance was impenetrable.

The plan was not to be. The Arianni had already anticipated possible actions from Goran and had instigated measures to assure that after Goran's spacecraft had activated their oxygen depletion weapon, the Arianni would immediately neutralize the act by its simple saltwater diversion system that the Arianni had developed eons ago to cleanse the Earth of any salt water intrusion to the sensitive middle Earth soil.

****

Back on Venus, Plotus and Roola were waiting for Goran. When Goran arrived with the nitrogen generator, they immediately seized it and arrested Goran. Anticipating Goran's return, Plotus announced to the population that Roola had replaced Goran as supreme sovereign. Roola then recalled all Annunaki space craft that were preparing to launch toward Earth to deploy the oxygen depletion weapon in a demonstration that could potentially cause untold deaths of surface humans.

With Goran in custody awaiting disposition, Roola contacted her Arianni friend Gunnar and invited him to come to Venus to assist in setting up the nitrogen generator. He would be of great use to the new sovereign of the Annunaki inasmuch as he helped design and test the generator.

"I would be delighted to come and assist you with the initiating process of the generator," Gunnar replied. "It will be wonderful to renew our relationship since those days when we were both sequestered in a prison cave. To reshape a new civilization would be exciting for both of us."

Gunnar examined his reflection in the azure tinted interior lake of Agartha. He imagined what life could be with Roola, now that the threat of an interplanetary war was over. It was something he knew he had to explore.

Chapter 14

RECOGNITION AND ACCOLADES

*T*he Galactic Alliance was formed eons ago to provide a confederation of planetary civilizations to monitor and enhance the peaceful co-existence of all Galactic neighbors. Their mission is to provide assistance to any group who continually promote peace, tolerance, and understanding by their commitment and actions. With its home base on the Jupiter moon Europa, one of the four largest of the huge planet's 79 moons,[1] the Alliance seeks to recognize those societies and individuals who, because of their actions, have taken uncommon steps to avoid confrontations between planetary cultures.

The Great Hall of Peace, built and nurtured by the regular contributions of all the planetary members, became, through tradition, the central location for accolade presentations to those who exhibited traits and actions that benefited peace and tranquility throughout the Galaxy. To be received with ceremony in this hall by the leaders of the Galactic community was a profound honor awarded to any civilization or individual(s) that exemplified the traditions held as sacrosanct.

The Alliance was led and coordinated by Malchiek, the well respected and chief operating officer of the group, who himself was the first recipient of the award due to his ability to form and keep the Alliance functioning through many challenging ordeals. He contacted Thal of the Arianni, after the near war with the Annunaki, to attend a ceremony on behalf of his Inner Earth populace for their extreme conscientiousness in not only averting an interplanetary war, but in striving to maintain the sanctity of all humanoids by restraining themselves from using lethal force. Their reluctance or refusal to use deadly force, protecting their own citizens and, concurrently, those of their potential enemy, impressed the entire alliance enough to propose a Galactic commendation for all those involved.

Tradition was to present to each individual who was instrumental in fulfilling the desires of the alliance with a golden crystal, with the feat recorded and placed in a crystal memory field that was accessible throughout the Galaxy.

As Malchiek took the podium to a resounding welcome, he looked around the enormous hall as he acknowledged each of the civilizations represented. Many different and varied humanoid representatives were present. The numbers attending the ceremony were astronomical, some in 3rd dimension bodies along with countless other light beings from the fifth dimension. All were here to honor, show respect, and give admiration to the awardees.

"It gives me great honor and pleasure to introduce to you the chief administrator for the Arianni, the culture and population of the Hollow Earth. He is the appointed representative of the General Counsel of Asgarth, the governing city of the Earth's interior. As is customary, he will introduce the recipients of our Galactic awards."

Thal walked on the galactic stage, aware that each civilization present looked forward to meeting and honoring the principal saviors of interior Venus, the surface of the Earth and the confines of the Hollow Earth, as well as recognizing their contribution to galactic peace. Each knew that such efforts mightily contributed to maintaining the efforts of peace and served to continually remind them of the vigor needed to maintain their own tranquility in their own civilizations.

"Greetings fellow beings," began Thal, "This is a great day for all the inhabitants of both Earth and Venus. It is a time for praise, recognition and thankfulness to those who actively work and contribute to peace. The recipients here are well deserving of any accolades they receive, but because they worked with their hearts, their greatest reward will be the legacy they have left behind. And each of them realizes that their work will begin anew when they return home. Our work on our own planet is a job in progress. Let me acknowledge them by having them join me on stage."

With those words Garrett, Gugga, Jared, Thora, Gunnar and Roola joined him.

"Who are they?" Thal asked rhetorically. "Let me take but a moment and introduce each to you and give you a quick synopsis of why they are receiving this august award.

"Initially, I want to recognize Ollie and Jackie Hill, who were the genesis of the original purpose to invoke the powers of the Holy Lance. They chose not to attend today in deference to their children. Their role, however, was to forge the pathway for the undertaking and they contributed greatly to the entire mission.

"And, in no particular order, are husband and wife, Garrett and Gugga Hill, son and daughter-in-law of Ollie and Jackie. These surface dwellers left the security and confines of the Earth surface world to retrieve the Holy Lance and return it to the Arianni at great personal risk. They continued as warriors assisting the Arianni in avoiding a major inter-planetary war between Earth and Venus. I cannot begin to list all of their contributions, but suffice it to say that they were critical and essential to the success of our joint mission.

"Critical is a word that doesn't fully capture what he did, but as a surface dweller turned Arianni through our acculturation process,

Jared Hill served as a leader in our space fleet to thwart many emergencies that only he, as a converted Arianni, could do.

"Raggs Raggnesson, along with Jared's son and Arianni born Gunnar, were the brains and inventors of the nitrogen generator that was instrumental and essential in saving the population of the Annunaki of interior Venus, who before this generator's operation, seemed to be doomed to extinction.

"It also gives me great pleasure to introduce Roola, now the chief sovereign of the Venetian Annunaki who, after her father, Molea's, death, became the calm, active, and brave direct voice to encourage negotiation and avoid confrontation. Her role was essential to the success of averting a planetary catastrophe. Her leadership of the Annunaki has restored the peaceful integration of the reptilian humanoids with the rest of the Galaxy. I also want to express our gratitude and appreciation to Thora, Solaris and Meda for contributing the key in solving the fractal formula for the nitrogen generator. It could not have been accomplished without their sojourn to Iceland and their combined revelation that unlocked the power of the Runic Triangle.

"Finally, let me introduce Thora, the latest holder of the Holy Lance, who because of her bravery, thoughtfulness, love and talents, has re-established the power of the Holy Lance and will soon begin a new chapter of history with the surface dwellers of the planet Earth.

"These are the recipients of the Golden Crystal award. They would be the first to acknowledge the assistance of many others, and they have expressed their gratitude in so many ways that are impossible to list.

"Let's give a warm, loving recognition and thankful blessing to these individuals for making us all proud. We owe you a debt of gratitude. Your legacy will live on forever in the annals of the Galactic Alliance."

To a thundering cacophony of enthusiastic response from the attendees, the recipients, one by one, stepped forward to receive their Golden Crystal, a treasured symbol of the power of goodness, gratitude, and victory.

****

The mood of the travelers during the trip back to Earth after such an overwhelming experience on Europa was somber, as each reflected on the gravity of everything that had taken place in these last months. Each humbly thanked Thal for his insistence on giving them commendation with such an award, bestowed in front of the many Galactic civilizations. Their gratefulness reflected the admiration they had for the Arianni leader who always carried a commitment to peace in his heart.

"Dad," Thora queried, "What will happen to Goran and the Captain?"

"Well," Garrett responded, "It appears that Goran will be subject to Venetian law and will, along with his cronies and co-conspirators, spend a substantial time in Annunaki custody, probably in a high security prison. I don't think that they will consider capital punishment. He probably also needs some mental health balancing as he had become consumed with megalomania. We have to remember that his early motivation was to save his planet, not necessarily to start a war. He went astray from there."

Garrett reflected a moment upon the fate of the Captain. "The Captain, my dear, is another story. Given the Arianni penchant for forgiveness and peace, their punishment might well be to have him ousted from the middle Earth and exiled to the surface world. I imagine he will then reconnect with the Knights and resume with them whatever it is they do in their quirky rituals.

"The Council also could choose to ban him from the planet entirely, perhaps to a far off Galaxy constellation such as Lyra or Vega. They might require him to return to his Source to learn the lessons of the elders in order to rebuild his spiritual awareness. I don't know, but the Supreme Council of Agartha will decide his fate."

Thora pondered her father's thoughts and dismissed from her mind any concern she might have for the grandfather she never knew. She trusted that he would learn his lessons in a way that was foreign to her, especially with the new role she was poised to step into.

Garrett and Thora both knew that their real work was just beginning. A host of problems on the Earth's surface were looming, with perhaps the most critical the threat posed by the proliferation of nuclear weapons. Of equal import were the ramifications of unbridled climate change and the repercussions of greed and uncontrolled population growth – each potentially triggering annihilation of both the surface world and Inner Earth. These issues would be paramount in their attention for years to come.

---

[1] With 79 moons revolving around Jupiter, the largest planet by far in the Earth's solar system, it is sometimes considered a solar system within itself.

Chapter 15

BRAVE NEW WORLD

*T*he experience with the Galactic Alliance and the gravity of the awards were still turning in their minds when Garrett, Gugga, Raggs, and Thora gathered the next week for a relaxing dinner. Thora was in a reflective mood trying to decipher in her mind and heart the lessons the Arianni had taught in their acculturation classes. She mused about what the other dimensions were like; what it takes to realize and be aware of other dimensions. She recognized that she possessed gifts that most other people did not have. Thora's intense listening to the language of the stones, hearing their meanings and acting as the conveyor of their guidance, was comfortable to her, but she had difficulty understanding where that guidance came from, and why to her?

She and her mom, Gugga, could often share mental telepathy at any distance and, in fact, Thora communicated with her mother often when Gugga was within the Inner Earth.

"Where did that all come from?" she mused.

And then there was her occasional clairvoyance, another gift she shared with her mother perhaps, yet again, from another lifetime or another dimension. All of this was now challenging her meditations and her third dimensional roots.

"Dad," she asked quizzically, "Why am I able to do these other-dimensional things when others can't? Do I possess a special gene that allows me to be so different from others?"

Garrett set down the technical manual he was studying and listened intently to his daughter's dilemma. He and Gugga had always known her capacity for inexplicable feats. They purposely waited until Thora would bring it up so as not to think she was so different and would label herself as weird. It appeared that Thora was now looking at herself with a new set of eyes.

"Well," Garrett began, "Your mother and I always knew you had these gifts and we knew at some point you would want to talk to us about them. I'm not sure I can give you a plausible answer, but I can share with you some of my own experiences as I'm sure Mom would be happy to do so as well."

"What do you mean?" Thora asked, "Do you and Mom have these same gifts? How did you know and what prompted them to reveal themselves?"

Garrett began a deep reflection of his own experiences. No, he didn't have the same gifts as Thora and her mother, but nonetheless had experiences that, even to this day, have challenged his thought and awareness.

He emerged from his thoughtful stupor and gazed at Thora with his own wondering eyes.

"I have had some clairvoyant experiences," he began.

"One, in particular, happened when I was being ordained as a Teutonic Knight. That was a new and entirely confusing moment when something reached within me and gave me a clear – not logical, – but a clear understanding of past life experiences that pertained to that moment in time. I didn't know what the experience was, but I knew instantly what it meant. It has permeated my thoughts ever since that time."

"What was the experience? How and why do you think it occurred?" posed Thora.

"You were, of course, a young and aware young lady at that time, but I was essentially held captive by the Knights even as I felt within that I was independent and free. But I wasn't free, and didn't realize it until I was faced with the 13 Knights in their historical garb at Wewelsburg Castle and brought into an occult ritual that took me out of my natural mind. I was mesmerized by the ritual and my mind flashed back through history as the image of the Holy Lance danced in front of me. I'll never forget it. My whole sense of reality was changed and I recognized each and every one of the Knights as they morphed into their historical bodies. Your grandfather, Otto, was standing next to me as my sponsor and I watched his face change, morph, into the gristly image of Adolf Hitler. I tried to evade the image but as I looked around, each Knight had also morphed into an evil image. Somehow, I seemed to grasp that I was being taken to a new dimension, a new reality, even as I realized that I was observing what was happening in this, the third dimension. I was able to hold my emotions as I drifted back and forth through this and the alternate dimension. It was then I recognized that I was surrounded by evil and had to maintain my emotional equilibrium in order not to alert the Knights as to my sudden change of heart."

"Wow, what an experience!" recoiled Thora as she reached out to grasp the hand of her father, sweating in obvious turmoil and confusion as to his own clairvoyance.

"Yeah," responded Garrett. "You can say that I also have experienced the magnitude of these gifts. But what I have realized is that I have experienced the revelation of my authentic self, and not the self that I project each day of my third dimensional life. Perhaps you are also becoming aware of your other dimensions of self. It appears that these dimensions exist concurrently with our third dimensional lives and challenge us to examine even further who we are and what we think we know. The only advice I can give you is to graciously and humbly accept your gifts and treat them as a precursor to new gifts that will unfold in the future. I believe that is what the Arianni are trying to teach us through their acculturation process – the ability to look within so we can become aware of who we actually are. The teachings tell us that we are more than our bodies, more than our thoughts, and more than our actions here in this third dimension. The only caveat to this comes when we think we have the answers, and spirit comes through and says, 'There's more.'"

"Yes, that actually makes some sense to me," Thora said to Garrett. "I never thought about it like that, but I feel I am being directed to rededicate myself to the acculturation teachings and seek to become what my destiny is revealing to me. Thank you, Dad, thank you for what you have shared. I love you so!"

****

The interior air was crisp and cool, somewhat of an anomaly for the Inner Earth climate. Garrett and Thora sat outside their bungalow with Raggs and Gugga enjoying the quiet of the safe surroundings when, unexpectedly, Sven appeared at the entrance. His normally relaxed manner seemed to be overridden by a bleak countenance as he greeted the group grimly.

"Sven," responded Garrett, "Please come and sit with us, you seem so gloomy. Is there something wrong?"

Sven hesitated for a moment, wanting to embrace his two friends, but it was clear he had something on his mind that was distracting him from his normal effervescent personality.

"I have some grave news," he mumbled. "There has been a nuclear detonation on the surface that, I fear, has cost some lives of the human population. We are responding to the incident as we speak, but it appears that some of the surface dwellers have crossed a critical line.

We don't know the extent or circumstances or who or what caused the explosion, but it has seriously disrupted the relatively peaceful aura of the surface."

"What!" cried Thora. "Have the Earth dwellers gone mad? What should we do?"

Raggs quickly embraced Thora as he felt her distress.

"We are doing all we can at the moment," replied Sven. "Our aerial patrols have been put on alert and we have sent our squadrons to survey and monitor the situation in case it is an attack among nations that would invite some kind of retaliation. We hope we are not witnessing the beginning of a surface nuclear war."

Raggs was frozen in disbelief. He never dreamed he would be witnessing such a cataclysmic event. His eyes danced wildly at the alarming reactions of his companions. Gugga quickly embraced Thora and Garrett knowing what such an occurrence could mean to their very existence. All were visibly upset by the news.

"Let's get back to central command," directed Garrett. "We have to find out what is going on."

Thora and Garrett locked eyes, both fearing that the long dreaded Armageddon had begun. They realized that their lives were now filled with incalculable challenges. Their relationship with the Holy Lance was now being initiated and the moment they had known was coming was now before them. Father and daughter held one another tightly, seeking comfort as they grasped that the future was now thrust upon them and they would play an important role in its unfolding.

Thora stepped away by herself to gain some perspective, gazing thoughtfully at the reflections of the golden inner sun off the nearby subterranean lake. The colors of the spectrum seemed to disperse themselves into seven distinct segments, each promising a new beginning.

"I will dedicate my life to service each day," she pledged solemnly to herself. "I will learn how to integrate my conscious self and begin to realize that my authentic self is my true identity. I will use the power of the Holy Lance to the best of my ability to resurrect and protect the sanctity of the surface dwellers and guide them to adopt the principles of the acculturation path of the Arianni. I will help fulfill the promise of humanity. I will give my life if that is my destiny. I cannot fail."

Appendix I

HOLDERS OF THE HOLY LANCE IN HISTORY

1. The first holder of the Lance was **Longinus,** also known as Gaius Cassius, who on Friday, April 5th, in 33 AD used his Lance to pierce the side of Jesus, the Messiah, while he was still nailed to the cross to determine whether he was alive or dead. From that time on, the spear was transformed and known as the Holy Lance. The Lance was passed down through Longinus' descendants and the legend persisted for over 2000 years.

2. The importance of the Lance was reaffirmed in 286 AD when it was in the possession of **St. Maurice,** known as **Mauritius.** He was a direct descendant of Longinus, as the spear was passed down from generation to generation. He carried the spear not as a weapon, but as a symbol of his faith. He became commander of the Theban Legion and was sent to crush a revolt in Switzerland. When he found out that the enemy were Christians, he refused. The Emperor instructed him to destroy the Lance, denounce Christianity and embrace the Roman gods. The **Emperor Maximian** told them that one of ten would be beheaded. The first was Mauritius, holding the lance above his head. After that, one in ten were decapitated. The rest stepped forward and 6666 legionnaires volunteered to be beheaded. Every man met a martyr's death.

   Although **Maximian** was a bitter enemy of the Christians, he, along with co-emperor **Diocletion,** ordered the burning of the scriptures but could not carry out his own order to destroy the Lance. He carried it away, believing that it was indeed the weapon of gods who had brought about the voluntary deaths of the over 6000 legionnaires.

3. In 308 AD, Fausta, daughter of Maximian, married **Emperor Constantine the Great** (280-337) in 313 AD. The Lance was given to Constantine as a wedding present. Constantine initiated the evolution of the Roman Empire into a Christian state.

4. With some improbability, the Holy Lance next appeared in the hands of **Atilla the Hun**. The Lance was relinquished by Roman emperor **Theodosius II** in exchange for not sacking Constantinople. Atilla was invincible before acquiring the Lance but his campaign soon began to collapse. In frustration, he galloped his horse to the gates of Rome and hurled the Lance at the feet of the officers who had been sent out to surrender the city. Thus, the Lance saved the city because Atilla did not understand the use of its power.

5. The spear then passed through a series of Roman emperors without attracting much attention. It then appeared in Gaul possessed by Frankish general **Charles Martel (Charles the Hammer)** who wielded it when he defeated invaders that saved Christian France from the forces of Islam. The year was 732 AD.

6. The Holy Lance then passed into the hands of **Charlemagne the Great** (742-814 AD) who used it as a symbol of unification in consolidating nearly all Christian lands of Western Europe. He carried the Lance during 47 successful campaigns, always slept with it close at hand, and believed it was the source of his clairvoyance.

7. In due time, the Lance came into the possession of **Heinrich I, Duke of Saxony and King of Germany** (876 – 936). Heinrich (also known as Henry the Fowler), used the Lance to bring a nine year truce with the Magyars of Hungary.

8. At some point in his reign, Henry is believed to have presented the Lance to the **English king, Athelstan.** Athelstan wrote six codes of law designed to suppress theft and corruption, that mitigated punishment of young offenders and provide comfort for the destitute. Athelstan returned the Lance to Germany when his sister, Eadgita (Edith) married **Otto the Great,** son of Henry. The Lance was part of her dowry.

9. **Otto the Great (912-973)** German king and Holy Roman Emperor, carried the spear during the consolidation of the first Reich (empire). He solidified relations between the Eastern and Western empires by

marrying his son, Otto II to the Byzantine princess Theophano. **Otto II (955- 983)** inherited the Lance from his father and passed it on to his son, **Otto III (980 – 1002).**

10. After being crowned king of Germany, Otto III managed to have his cousin elected as Gregory V, the first German Pope. Gregory, in turn, appointed **Otto III as emperor of the Holy Roman Empire in 996 AD.** Otto III proceeded to make Rome his headquarters and planned to recreate the glory of the Caesars. He regarded himself as the leader of world Christianity. During his reign, a nail from the cross was inserted into the holy spear. The metal was weakened and a fracture occurred. The two parts were fitted with an iron clamp designed to hold them together. (The imitation Lance of Krakow was also created at about this time).

11. **Henry II, the Saint (973 – 1024)** seized the Lance and the insignia of the German kings and Holy Roman emperors on the occasion of the death of Otto III. By this time the insignia included a crown, globe, scepter, sword, cross, gauntlet, and other precious items.

12. The Lance was then passed on to **Henry III (1017 - 1056)** who in turn left it to his son, **Henry IV (1050 – 1106).** Henry IV had the Lance fitted with a silver sleeve which bore a Latin inscription. A golden sleeve was added at a later date (the silver was replaced with gold during the reign of *Charles IV of Bohemia (1316 – 1378)*. Both attachments bore the Latin words "Clavus Dominicus," (the nail of our Lord).

13. One of the more interesting chapters of this history took place after the Lance came into the possession of **Frederick I Barbarossa (Redbeard) in 1123 – 1190.** He was the king of Germany and Holy Roman Emperor. Barbarossa was the son of Frederick, Duke of Swabia, of the House of Hohenstaufen. His long career was closely entwined with that of *Duke Henry the Lion of Saxony*. Frederick became a legendary hero and a symbol of unity to the German people. In the spring of 1189, Frederick answered the call to the Third Crusade to free Jerusalem from occupation by Saladin's army and to recover the "true cross."

He formed, along with *Duke of Swabia and Duke Leopold of Austria (1159 – 1194)*, the largest Crusade army to that date and set out for the Holy Lands by an overland route. **Barbarossa** carried the Holy Lance as his emblem of faith and Christian dedication. The Lance did not protect him as he drowned (1190) while trying to cross the Saleph River in what is now Turkey. Under the other two Dukes, the force reached Palestine which brought the Lance back home to its place of origin – over 1000 years later.

14. After the siege and capture of the city of Acre in 1191, **Leopold** quarreled with the powerful *King Richard of England* and decided that the Lance should be hidden in some secret place. In that year, a secret organization of crusaders formed the Teutonic Knights, or **Knights of the Teutonic Order**. Leopold placed the lance in their custody. Richard of England forced Leopold to quit the Crusade and come home.

15. The Teutonic Knights assumed a military character in 1198 under their grand master, **Hermann von Salza (1210 – 1239)**. The lance went with them and served as their banner of faith during the conquest and Christianization of Prussia. During the reign of **Frederick the II (1194 – 1250)**, grandson of *Frederick Barbarrosa*, the Mongols threatened Europe from the East under the successors of Genghis Khan. The Teutonic Knights felt that the Lance would be safer if removed to western Germany. They returned it along with other insignia of the Holy Roman Empire.

16. Nothing very dramatic appeared in the history of the Lance for the next 550 years. By 1806, Napoleon had overrun most of Europe and brought the first Reich to an end, after it had endured for over 1,000 years. He dissolved the order of the Teutonic Knights, but did not fall heir to the insignia of the German kings and Holy Roman Emperors. The Lance and its companion pieces were hidden in an ancient tunnel beneath the ramparts of Nuremburg castle. However, there was still concern that the treasure might be found by Napoleon, and so it was sent to Vienna, Austria for safe keeping.

17. The Lance was received by **Francis II**, who had been forced to abdicate as *the last of the Holy Roman Emperors,* but was still **Emperor of Austria**. Thus it was passed into possession of the lords of the House of Hapsburg and placed in the treasure room of the ancestral palace, The Hofburg, in Vienna. After Napoleon lost power in 1814, German authorities requested that the treasure be returned. They met with considerable resistance, although the Austrian Empire did reinstitute the order of the Teutonic Knights in 1834. In Vienna, the Lance rested after its long journey through the first Reich.

18. More to this journey. By 1795 the shaft of the Lance was detached and left behind. The shaft was later transferred to the Vatican where it can presently be viewed.

19. Adolf Hitler first encountered the Lance of Longinus in 1907. It was his source of mystic inspiration for the rest of his life. It passed from his hands in 1945 and was secreted in an ice cave in Deutsche Antarctica. It was subsequently brought back to Germany by a contingent of Teutonic Knights in 1978 and is held in a secret location by the Order of the Teutonic Knights.

From *The Return of the Holy Lance* by Wilhelm Bernhart, limited edition published by Dan Weiss, 1985.

Appendix II

Runes/The Runic Triangle

Runes are an alphabetic system that predated Latin and were symbols inscribed on stone or wood. They appeared only vertically or at an angle because horizontal lines cut into substances could crack wooden or rock scriptures. The earliest 24 runes dated from 150 AD and were known as the Elder Futhark. There are two additional rune groups called the Anglo-Saxon Futhark (400 – 1100 AD) and the Younger Futhark (800 – 1100 AD). The earliest runic inscriptions remain a linguistic mystery. Because of this mystery, early runes were not employed as a writing system, but rather were used as tools for divination. *Rune* means secret or something hidden, the knowledge of which is esoteric or restricted to an elite. Modern (1980) versions include a blank rune, said to represent "The Unknowable."

The Runic Triangle does not appear in any folklore. However the runic signs, arranged as a triangle, can release a force or frequency that can open locked doors, tombs, caves and caverns – or in this case, can generate information to complete a scientific puzzle. The placement of a particular energizing stone into the center of the triangle is necessary to activate its power. In this case, the same curious pebble of extraterrestrial origin that appears in book one serves as the energizer for activating the triangle.

The Runic triangle that provided the missing piece of the puzzle of the nitrogen generator was made up of the following runes: The first rune, as received in Meda's vision, was placed at the top of the triangle. It was Number 14 – KANO, which is the Rune of Opening and renewed clarity. The second rune was number 17 – EHWAZ, placed to the bottom left of the triangle form. Ehwaz is a Rune of Progress, spurring movement in the sense of improving or bettering any situation. The final rune, completing the triangle, was number 22 – DAGAZ which is the rune of Breakthrough, signaling a major shift or radical transformation.

Appendix III

EVOLUTION OF THE HUMANOIDS

Questions always arise as to how the hollow middle Earth dwellers got here, Why are they similar and yet different? Surface humans ponder the same dilemma. Who are we? Where did we come from? Why do we look like we look? The following is an attempt to explain some of the history of the humanoid and how we, the surface humans came to be.[1]

The evolution of the bipedal humanoid is rooted within the Galaxy, indeed within the entire universe. Each individual humanoid species has the same general characteristics such as a torso, head, two arms and two leg appendages. Most, however, diverge from the general traits to exhibit different shapes, sizes, skin type, color, and other unique features. The Earth humanoid shares with all of them much of the same DNA even as other strands may appear in their composition.[2] There are varying species within the humanoid prototype that may be physically smaller or somewhat larger than humans or differ in head sizes or other features in relation to the rest of their body. All, however, share the same genetic history within the universe.

The creators of humanoids were known as the Founders or Elders. They represented Source or the concept of God. They existed from a white hole from a White Star which provides a prism of light through which passed the first humanoids into existence, the inhabitants of Lyra, the mother constellation. The light split into the familiar color spectrum created seven densities. This was the beginning of creation involving the humanoid form. Each density represented the physical and spiritual station in each individual humanoid and how it exists and functions. Most of us here on planet Earth exist in the third dimension, while those in the Hollow Earth are concurrent travelers to and from the 5th dimension and higher. All are striving for integration, a concept of returning to our oneness, to our Source or God.

The birthplace of the bipedal humanoid is rooted in the constellation Lyra. Lyra is the mother star for all humanoids that exist in the Galaxy. From Lyra, various groups have broken away in a process called *fragmentation*. This process is a much like the biological event known as mitosis where the main structure of an amoeba divides in two, creating a new animal. The difference is that in fragmentation the split is not a physical body split but rather a psychological and spiritual split. Groups of Lyrans had differences and chose to leave Lyra and form a new civilization on yet another solar system.

In tracing the fragmentation of Lyra, the first new colony was the star Vega which became a growing civilization with another point of view, a different perspective and polarity as to how the civilization should be constructed and managed. Vega became the opposite polarity of what Lyra represented and thrived with a new philosophy. It was only natural that the factions on Vega also began to fragment and that portion of the civilization moved to the third star of the constellation, Apex.

Each of these fragmentations divided humanoids into smaller groups with differing characteristics and physical anomalies from our current Earth human countenance. Over the eons the varying species, although still humanoid with humanoid characteristics, took different shapes, sizes and general appearances. While the Apex fragmentation represented a neutral polarity from Lyra and Vega, the Apexian civilization was rampant with power, greed and jealousy. It did not survive as its power and greed proved fatal to the planet and was thus devastated by destruction and war with nuclear implications. A small number of inhabitants secured themselves underground, but the remainder perished from their own inability to integrate with one another.

Meanwhile, the Lyran races and the Vegan civilizations were continuing with their development. The Lyrans wanted to remove themselves from the friction with the Vegans and sought out many other areas to colonize. Groups of Vegans also sought other areas of colonization. Humanity was spreading rapidly carrying with the seeds of experience and polarity. Gone were the clear-cut lines of traceable philosophic and genetic history.

Buried deeply in the souls of all, the goal of integration of each being pushed them onward. The ultimate goal still being integration – a lesson continually presented but never achieved. This proved to the Founders that integration was subject to the free will of each individual and the entire galactic family could only wait, knowing that in chaos there is order – divine order. The Founders still wait silently. They exist not only in the white light but also within the soul of humanity as its most basic archetype.

Perhaps the lesson is in the archetype, one which is so obvious that it is not easily perceived. The founders whisper through the expanse of time and dimension. The founders wait patiently for humankind to heed the call of integrated evolution inasmuch as the cycle of life and existence is merely a circle; the beginning and end are the same.

We can further trace the sojourn of mankind by understanding the effect of Sirius, the tertiary star group. This realm was the first to be explored by the curious consciousness that passed through the prism of Lyra and fragmented from the Founders. The Triad represents the polarity templates, two polarities at the base of the triangles, and the joining or integrating of the polarities at the apex. It represents the basic foundation of the galactic family's desire – to once again unify through the merging of polarities. The differing polarities of Lyra and Vega clashed again in Sirius as both sought to establish a spiritual teaching to their liking. They decided to move their conflict to another locale as the elders of Sirius finally intervened. The discovered the electromagnet properties of the area called Orion. Once the conflict had been removed from the Sirius system, the physical civilization remained having cut themselves off from spirit. Those desiring the negative positive integration went to Orion instead of Sirius. Other positives from Lyra joined the Orion struggle. Thus galactic history was born.

Perhaps the most notable step for the understanding of humanoid evolution was the realm of Arcturus. The positive polarities of Sirius, oriented to facilitate healing, had allied themselves with the energies of Arcturus which was oriented towards the idea of emotional healing. Together they formed the Sirius/Arcturus matrix which has found its way onto nearly every physical plane within the galactic family as a holistic energy representing body, mind, and spirit. It is from here that the planet Earth becomes a part of the matrix. It is an archetypal energy that is used by an individual or society for many purposes. It is malleable and can be shaped into any appropriate definition. Whatever the shape, it is devoted to the service of physicality. The Sirius/Arcturus Matrix reminds the varying fragments of their connection to the Whole and their natural abilities for self-healings.

So how did we get here? Although only a small percentage, a group of positive Sirians decided to incarnate into physicality as well. However they rejected the humanoid form for a form that is more representative of their nature. This form is the Cetacean – dolphins and whales.

1   For more detailed information and knowledge of the evolution of our species, consult *The Prism of Lyra*, by Lyssa Royal and Keith Priest. Their channeling of the history of mankind is a detailed study of where we come from within the Galaxy and why we are here. Much of the information specified here is gleaned from their studies. It chronicles in detail the emergence of the reptiles in humanoid form, such as the Annunaki, the Venetian middle dwellers. Much of the dialog of this chapter is gleaned from their research and writing. I highly recommend the reading! Also, see appendix 5 for more discussion.

2   For example, there are Reptoids who have rough, scaly skin, have a different color hue and, perhaps, a different respiratory system requiring fluctuating amounts of oxygen, nitrogen, or other atmospheric gases. They are, however, the results of Vegan experimentation with gene splicing that proved a creation of a new species. Reptiles, at that time were the only other DNA forms that were available. There exist today Vegan Reptilians and Vegan Mammalians.